Seth won't be responsible for two defenseless women on his wagon train.

She stopped and turned, and her eyes flared wider. Instantly, a soft vulnerability in her features disappeared behind a facade of purposeful determination. "Oh, it's you."

"Who'd you expect?" he spat, instantly regretting his harsh tone. "Look, take the—" Conscious of the intense interest of a growing number of passersby, Seth knew better than to wag a handful of cash out in the open, and instead slid the bank notes back within the confines of his jacket pocket. Then he grabbed Amanda Shelby's elbow, ignoring the mortification which glared at him from her narrowed eyes, and steered her to an unoccupied spot a short distance away. There he turned her to face himself. "Please, Miss Shelby. I've been called blunt at times and have probably hurt a few feelings in my day, so if I'm hurting yours I'm sorry. But you don't seem to understand. The journey west is grueling, even for tough, experienced folks, and some of the hardiest souls won't survive it, let alone a couple gals like you and your sister."

"I don't believe that."

"Do you know how to shoot?"

"No, but—"

"Can you change a wheel? The trail rattles the best wagon to shambles."

"No."

"How about repairing harness?"

The last thing he was prepared for was the sheen of tears which glazed her eyes before she lowered them in defeat.

SALLY LAITY is an accomplished writer of both contemporary and historical romances and has firmly established herself in the inspirational romance field.

Books by Sally Laity

HEARTSONG PRESENTS
HP4—Reflections of the Heart
HP31—Dream Spinner
HP81—Better than Friends

Valiant
Heart

Sally Laity

Heartsong Presents

DEDICATION
To Barb,
my forever friend.

ACKNOWLEDGEMENT
My profound gratitude to Gloria Brandt, Dianna
Crawford, and Edwina Harlander. . .this couldn't have
been done without you. May the Lord bless you all.

A note from the author:
*I love to hear from my readers! You may write to me at
the following address:*   **Sally Laity**
Author Relations
P.O. Box 719
Uhrichsville, OH 44683

ISBN 1-57748-151-8

VALIANT HEART

Cover illustration by Randy Hamlin.

PRINTED IN THE U S A.

Valiant Heart

By Sally Laity

The first time I laid eyes on you
  I thought you were like all the others. . .
Helpless, weepy, and a lot less bright than you should be.
  How wrong I was.
For what I perceived to be
  A stubborn streak turned out to be the opposite. . .
Fortitude. Backbone.
  A spirit of adventure.
Yet despite those admirable traits,
  What struck me most about you
Were things entirely different. . .
  Qualities I could not even name, at first.
Trust. Hope. Striving onward for what is right.
  I see now that faith is something
Which stretches beyond Sunday
  to all the days of one's life.
And character comes from deep within. . .
  As intangible and enduring as a valiant heart.

one

Missouri
May 1848

Amanda Shelby stared out the window of her second-story room in the Bradford Hotel. Scattered showers had dotted the dirt streets of Independence with puddles—glossy brown mirrors that reflected the puffy clouds and blue expanse of the ever-changing spring sky above.

And everywhere were people. Young and old, whole families of them, eager and waiting to start out on the trail to the rich, fertile valleys and hills of Oregon. They had all but emptied the mercantile and hardware stores of goods until new shipments arrived, and then those, too, would be snatched up before they had time to gather dust on the shelves. The process would repeat itself over and over throughout the spring as numerous companies of travelers gathered to begin the westward trek over mountains and plains to establish new homes before the onset of winter.

As she gazed wistfully at the bustling scene below, the iron-rimmed wheels of a pair of Conestogas splashed through the puddles, rumbling toward the growing encampment near the spring on the outskirts of town. Two small boys leaned precariously out of the bowed canvas top of the second wagon, their eyes round with excitement. At the sight of a garishly dressed woman in red satin and a feather boa, in front of the Bluebird Saloon, they elbowed each other, then darted back inside the confines of their arched haven.

Amanda released a sigh and steeled her heart against a twinge of sadness. Only a few short weeks ago, Pa had driven her and Sarah Jane in their own prairie schooner over the quay and up the steep grade to Independence Square, their hearts full of hopes and plans for the trip overland to the Far West. But that seemed so long ago, almost like a dream. Nothing could alter the grim reality that Pa now occupied a fresh grave on a lonely hillside a mere stone's throw away. The cruel twist of fate had brought a swift end to the visions of their wondrous new life. Now the world felt bleak and empty, and Amanda had no idea what she and Sarah would do.

Almost as if the last thought had been an audible summons, her seventeen-year-old younger sister breezed into the room, wheat-gold curls slightly tangled by the breeze. The triumphant smile that lit her guileless face looked a little out of place against the shadows beneath her eyes. Amanda had been more than aware of Sarah's tossing and turning each night during the past few weeks—and her soft crying. But during her waking hours the younger girl flitted about in a near frenzy of activity, as if trying to keep too busy to dwell on their losses.

Sarah draped her woolen shawl over the back of a chair and held out her tote. "There were only three bottles of sarsaparilla left in the whole town! I nearly had to fend off a mob to get one of them!" Then she sobered, concern drawing her fine brows together above shimmering eyes of clearest blue. "Something wrong, Mandy?"

"Just thinking a little too much." Amanda silently regarded her sibling, who was the very picture of what she herself had always wished to be—willowy and graceful as Mama, with delicate features and a face that never failed to turn heads. But alas, that particular dream had been in vain. Amanda had conceded long ago that it was only fair that one of them resembled the plainer, sturdier Shelby side of the family, and she was the only other one there was. Twisting an errant strand of light auburn hair absently between her thumb and forefinger, she backed away from the muslin-curtained window and sank to a chair, smoothing the skirt of her somber brown cotton dress.

Sarah set down her booty on the small round table next to the door, then crossed the room and gave Amanda a hug. "As Mama always said, death is as much a part of life as birth is." She made a wry grimace, and when she spoke again, her tone sounded tart. "Maybe we should be used to it by now, after losing everyone dearest to us this past year."

Yes, everyone. Shaking off the tormenting reminder that her own losses went beyond mere beloved family members— to the death of her most cherished dream as well—Amanda quickly snuffed the thoughts that could so easily consume her in bitterness. "I'll never ever be used to it."

The younger girl smiled gently and gave Amanda's shoulder a comforting squeeze. "No, I don't suppose I will either, to be truthful. But at least we can think on what Pa said just before he passed on, about not wanting us to wear black and drown in mournful tears. He felt his time had come, and he had peace about where he was going. And he's with Mama now. Her and the baby. As for us, well, I think we owe it to him to heed his words and keep alive his dream of starting over."

"Whatever you say." Pressing her lips tightly together before she voiced a thought about the senselessness of life, Amanda heard a growing noise outside. She stood and returned to the window to see a handful of rowdy boys wrestling in the soggy dirt on the street below. Not far from them, two shaggily dressed buffalo hunters with clenched fists were in a heated debate of their own, their gruff voices spewing bursts of profanity to which no one paid the slightest heed.

From the corner of her eye, Amanda could see her sister filling two tall glasses.

Sarah offered one to her as she stepped to her side. "What's all the commotion?"

"Another fight. I'm looking forward to some peace and quiet when that train finally pulls out."

"So am I. Surely the spring grasses along the route are green and tall enough for the animals to graze on by now."

Several minutes of silence lapsed as they sipped their drinks and surveyed the harried activity that seemed never to cease. Independence, far from being a sleepy little hamlet, was second only to St. Louis as a river port. The hotel proprietor had assured them that the height of each spring season was the same—the whole town overrun with river men, steamship captains, hunters and trappers, traders, teamsters, and hordes of emigrants, the latter all fighting over the scant grazing for their thousands of horses, mules, and oxen. Even on the Lord's Day, constant movement and voices of the transients filled the air.

"What do you think will become of us?"

Amanda caught her breath. She had been wondering the very same thing herself. Staying at the hotel indefinitely was not even a remote possibility. The expense of lodging and meals was putting a serious drain on their funds and would soon make it necessary for them both to seek employment. The home and possessions that had been sold before leaving the verdant green woods of northeastern Pennsylvania now seemed not only part of some other world, but another life as well.

Unbidden memories of sailing the Great Lakes to Chicago, then boarding a steamboat to St. Louis and securing their outfit for going west, were as real in her mind as if they had occurred yesterday. Who would have imagined all of that would come to naught, all Pa's plans to relocate in Oregon Territory and use his woodcrafting talents to provide for the three of them. Now it was left to Amanda and her sister to make their own life somewhere. Somehow.

Sarah Jane stepped away from the window and moved to the dark pine four-poster abutting one wall of the room. She picked up her guitar from where it leaned against the headboard. After absently twisting the tuning pegs and adjusting the pitch, she sat down on the quilted counterpane and strummed a soft chord, then another, and a dreamy smile curved her lips.

Amanda groaned inwardly. Strumming always led to singing, and for all Sarah's innocent sincerity and melodious speaking voice, she was blissfully unaware of the fact she could not carry a tune. "I, um, think I'll go for a walk and get the cobwebs out of my head," Amanda blurted. She grabbed her gloves and warm shawl from the armoire and made a swift exit on the first few hummed notes.

Outside, the soles of Amanda's hightop shoes made hollow sounds on the board sidewalk, the rhythmic echoes blending with the voices and footfalls of others as she threaded her way through the throng, dodging loose chickens and the occasional small farm animal in her path. False fronts on the assorted wooden buildings lining both sides of the street gave the illusion they were more impressive than they actually were. After passing the bank and the barber, the wheelwright and gunsmith, she finally stopped at the last smithy's shop on the street.

The owner, a stocky, muscular man in his mid-forties, glanced up from the red-hot horseshoe he was plucking from the fire with a pair of long tongs. "Afternoon, miss." He nudged the beak of his black working cap higher, exposing a band of light skin on his soot-streaked forehead.

"Good afternoon, Mr. Plummer. No one has purchased the wagon as yet?"

" 'Fraid not. Folks what need 'em, already has 'em by the time they get to town, unless they arranged ahead of time for one of the wagonwrights to build 'em one." He set the glowing shoe down on the anvil and raised a muscled arm to administer a few whacks with his hammer.

Amanda's ears rang with each blow, and she sighed as she gazed at the big wagon Pa had bought, now parked alongside the enterprise. Such a waste, brand spanking new, and complete with foodstuffs and tools sufficient for the journey west, plus three braces of mules being housed in the livery. Surely someone should have been interested in it by this time. It galled her to think she might end up having to sell the entire outfit to that shrewd Mr. Cavanaugh, the owner of the mercantile, after all. The offer he had made for it was shockingly low—despite the ridiculous prices he charged for things in his store. The knowledge that her and her sister's loss would be very profitable to that scoundrel was a bitter pill to swallow. Amanda could just picture his smug expression of triumph if she were forced by circumstance to acquiesce. "Well, I'll check back with you tomorrow," she said, turning to leave. "Perhaps someone will still come along and want it."

"Could be. I did have a couple of people askin' after the goods." He cocked a bushy eyebrow in question.

Amanda shook her head. "No. We wouldn't want to sell things off that way except as a last resort. Certainly a full wagon would be of much more value to a latecomer, don't you think? We've been careful to leave everything intact so the entire outfit would be available for a quick sale."

" 'S'pose there's always that possibility, but time's runnin' out, miss, till the next train starts gatherin'."

"I'm aware of that. But still. . ."

He sniffed and wiped his bulbous nose with a large kerchief, then returned the cloth to his back pocket. "Well, don't worry, I won't do nothin' without your say-so. I'm keepin' an eye on it for ya."

"Thank you, Mr. Plummer. My sister and I truly appreciate all your trouble. Good day."

With a heavy heart and at a much slower pace, she strolled toward the hotel. Slanting rays of the sun at Amanda's back elongated her shadow as it flowed gracefully over the walk ahead, making her appear several inches taller than her five-foot height—and nearly as slender as Sarah. She lifted her chin.

Several hours later, kneeling at her bedside, Amanda did her best to ignore the outside racket while she formulated her heavenly petitions. When the cool breath of night rustled the curtain on the partially open bedroom window and raised gooseflesh, she rose and climbed into the warm bed.

"Your prayers took longer than usual," Sarah said.

"I have a lot on my mind," Amanda confessed.

All at once her sister's seemingly blithe acceptance of their fate irked her. Blinking back stinging tears, she raised up on one elbow to face the younger girl, unable to bite back the angry words that insisted upon tumbling out of her mouth. "Aren't you the least concerned that we're completely alone in the world now—and have only a pittance to get us by for heaven knows how long? It took everything Pa could scrape together after paying off those debts that—that—" Amanda fought to keep from choking on the name, "*Morris Jamison* dumped on him, you know, to finance this venture. And when our money is gone, I haven't the slightest idea what we're going to do."

"I never said I wasn't concerned," Sarah said quietly.

Chagrined at the sight of the moisture glistening in her sister's eyes, Amanda berated herself for her hasty words and reached over to hug Sarah. "I know. I'm sorry, Sissy. I shouldn't have said that."

"The Reverend O'Neill told us we have to trust God for the strength we need to go on. And the more I think about it, the more I agree. We can't spend the rest of our lives moping around, however tempting that might be. Pa did that after Mama died, and look what it did to him. Working day and night, not sleeping, barely eating. . ."

"Yes, you're right."

"It's no wonder his malaria came back again—only this time he wasn't strong enough to fight it off. Even if we still have days when we're so sad we can't think straight, we have to keep living. And whatever pit of trouble we're in now, we have to climb out of it ourselves, no matter what." She folded her arms over her bosom. "So I'm going to apply myself to finding a husband—one handsome and rich—so I can get as much as I can out of life."

Amanda blinked, aghast. "And how do you plan to do that, exactly. . .if you don't mind my asking. No one has bought that stupid wagon yet, and we really need the money."

Sarah's quiet, even breaths made the only sound in the room for several seconds. "Things work out for the best, don't they? I figure the wagon didn't sell because we need it."

"I beg your pardon?" Amanda sat up in bed, the covers clutched in her hands as she stared through the dim light in her sister's direction.

"We need it. You and I. We're going to go west ourselves, the two of us."

two

Amanda's mouth fell open at her sister's statement. "That has got to be the most—" she fluttered a hand in speechless futility. "I'm surprised that even you could say such a dumb thing!"

Sarah Jane flinched and lowered her gaze.

Amanda knew her younger sister considered her pessimistic and staid, a stick-in-the-mud person, one who rarely gave the girl credit for having a sensible thought in her little blond head. But with both Pa and Mama gone and no one else left to them in this world, the crushing weight of responsibility Amanda felt made it almost impossible to temper her words. It was high time Sarah started acting more like the young woman she was than the little girl she still wished to be.

"It isn't dumb," Sarah said evenly. "Surely you can see this town is not a fit place for two unchaperoned girls. We left Pennsylvania to begin a new life out west, didn't we? Well, now that we've started in that direction, I think we should keep going."

Amanda could scarcely breathe. She stared toward the parted curtain panels, where the glow from outside cast silver outlines on the roofs across the street and glazed the edges of the furniture in the hotel room. She released a despondent huff and flopped back down on her pillow. "I just don't know. I truly don't."

Sarah, the contours of her slight body shrouded in blue-violet shadows and blankets, remained silent for a long moment as her tapered finger tapped the counterpane. "I picked some spring flowers today and took them out to Pa's grave. And something inside of me made me start singing— you know how he always loved my singing."

An inner smile struggled for release, but Amanda managed to contain it as her sister went on.

"Anyway, when my song was done, I asked him what we should do, where we should go. He always did give the best advice. And it came to me—as if Pa had said it himself—the wagon is bought and paid for. It has everything we need to go west just like we would have if he hadn't passed on. The least we can do is to try to see that dream of his through. He would want us to. We owe it to him."

Amanda didn't respond for several moments as her sister's preposterous notion warred in her mind. She gave a shaky sigh. "Know what really scares me?"

"Hm?"

"You could be right. I don't see any other choice for us at the moment. No matter where we go, we're going to be alone. We've got no one to go back to, and I sure don't want to settle in a place like this, full of ruffians and drifters." She paused again in deep thought. "If we did go west the way Pa wanted—and I'm not altogether sure we should, mind you— maybe it would feel like a part of him would be with us." She paused. "We might just find a good new life for our- selves. Those new woodworking tools of his could provide the resources we need for a while. Maybe even enable us to open a shop of our own in Oregon."

"What kind of shop?"

Unexpectedly, with the decision to go not actually settled yet, a feasible possibility came to mind. "If there's one worth- while thing Maddie managed to teach us it was how to use a needle. Think about it. More flocks of people are heading west all the time. And they'll all be in need of clothes. They'll have their hands so full trying to clear land and build homes before the onset of winter there won't be much time for less needful things, like sewing."

"Yes!" A growing excitement colored Sarah's breathless voice. "That's a grand idea. Truly grand! And we wouldn't have to wait to settle somewhere before we got started. We could buy some bolts of dry goods right here in Independence, then one of us could ride in back and sew bonnets and aprons and baby things while the other drove."

"Maybe. It's just a thought." Amanda, feeling the first flickers of doubt after her initial enthusiasm, needed time to ponder the idea before making a definite commitment that would alter their lives forever. Then she tossed caution to the wind. "I'll get in touch with the wagon master and make the arrangements to go with the train as planned."

Sarah Jane's teeth glistened like pearls in her wide grin, and Amanda couldn't help wondering what sort of unpredictable hopes and dreams were taking shape in her sister's imaginings. It would be one huge chore keeping the flighty girl in check during a long westward journey.

Nevertheless, in that brief instant, Amanda felt a tiny bit of Sarah's optimism course through her being, accompanied by an uncharacteristic surge of adventure. Maybe for once in her life Sarah was actually right. Heading west would be far better than letting sadness and grief defeat them. . .and besides, if they really put their minds to it, perhaps they truly could make a good life out there. A small smile tugged at her lips as she relaxed and closed her eyes, sloughing off the guilt from not having sought God's guidance in the matter.

&

Early the next morning, the crowing of the rooster out back awakened Amanda. The curtain of night had barely begun to lift, spreading a band of thin light outward from the eastern sky. She checked over her shoulder to see Sarah still in deep slumber. It was an opportune time to talk things over with the Lord.

Reaching for her flannel wrap, Amanda slipped her arms into it and tied the belt snugly, then knelt beside the bed. *Dear heavenly Father*, she prayed silently, desperately, *I don't*

*really know what to pray. Nothing has happened the way we
expected it to since we three came to Independence. And now
with Pa gone, Sarah and I have nowhere to turn. We can't go
back to the home we used to know, and it's a fact this town is
not a fit place for us to settle. We've decided to see to Pa's
wish and go west.*

She paused to gather her thoughts. *In truth, I don't know
how we'll manage this long journey alone, since neither of us
is used to doing for ourselves. Back home we had Maddie to
cook and keep things nice while we girls wiled away our time
in what I admit now were frivolous pursuits. But we're strong
and healthy, and we can learn. I know that for certain. Please
go with us on our way. Grant us wisdom and courage, and
stay close to us in the weeks ahead.*

When there were no words left inside, she rose and crawled
back into the warm bed again for a few more minutes of
sleep, thankful for the blankets that chased away the chill of
the early hour. She would have liked to have more inner
peace over her decision, but perhaps that would come in time.
Pa always said a person's steps were ordered by the Lord, and
circumstances had all but forced this plan upon them. Surely
it had to be God's will. Determined, she pressed her lips
together and closed her heavy eyelids as peace settled over
her like a quilt of down.

A short time later, Amanda awoke again to full morning
brightness. She dressed in her best navy worsted dress, confident that the tailored fit and fashionable sleeves made her
look older than her twenty years. After twisting her long hair
into a neat figure-eight coil at the nape of her neck, she added
her Sunday bonnet, tying a stylish bow just beneath her chin.

"You look divine," Sarah Jane gushed. "Ever so grown-up
and important."

"I'm trying very hard to convince myself I feel important,"
she confessed. "Let's go have breakfast, and then I'll try to
locate the man Pa made the arrangements with."

৵

At Martha's Eatery, a bustling restaurant popular with trail guides and mountain men alike, Seth Holloway shoved the empty plate away and leaned back in the chair, unfolding his cramped legs. He glanced across the table at rusty-haired Red Hanfield, his partner and longtime friend. "I had word that the O'Bradys pulled into town this morning. That's the last family we've been waiting for. I'll see they have all their supplies so we can head out day after tomorrow. You ride point with the first wagons this time, and I'll follow along with the cow column."

"Yep, just make sure you don't ride last in line," his wiry pal quipped. "Wastes a lot of time high-steppin' them cow pies." His coppery mustache twitched in barely suppressed humor.

"I get the picture," Seth grated. Picking up his coffee mug, he drained the last bit in one gulp, then set it back down.

"Ready for a refill?" At his elbow, good-natured Martha Griffith, owner and chief cook, poured a fresh cup.

"I do thank you, ma'am," Seth said, grinning up at her with admiration. No matter the time of day, the perky woman always sported a crisp, spotless apron over her calico dress, and the ruffle on her cap was always neatly starched over her salt-and-pepper bun. The two serving girls who worked for her were similarly attired. "You never let a man run dry."

"No sense in it a'tall, when the pot's always on! I like to make sure my regulars always come back."

"As if anybody else in town cooks as good as you," Red piped up.

Martha's pink cheeks dimpled with a smile as she filled his cup also. "Mighty kind words for a busy woman. I knew there was a reason I always like to see you two comin' in off the prairie." With a cheery dip of her head, she continued making the rounds with the coffeepot.

Seth observed her efficient movements absently as he slowly drank the hot liquid, his mind recounting endless last-minute details that needed his attention before the wagon train departed Independence two days hence.

On the edge of his vision he noticed a dark-clad figure approaching the table he and his pal occupied. He looked up when the rather small, smartly dressed young woman stopped beside them. Her classic features were composed in a businesslike expression, but it was her eyes that drew his like a magnet. Large and luminous, an unmistakable sadness lurked within their clear green depths.

"I beg your pardon?" she said softly.

"Miss?"

"I'm looking for Mr. Holloway."

They both rose at once. "That's me," Seth said, mentally noting some nicely rounded curves, neat, nearly auburn hair beneath a prim bonnet, a tempting but unsmiling mouth. "Seth Holloway. This is my partner, Red Hanfield. What might I do for you?" Noticing that her hands, gloved in white kid, trembled slightly despite her confident demeanor, he returned his gaze to her eyes, caught again by the cheerlessness accented by the fringe of long lashes.

She moistened her lips. "My name is Amanda Shelby. My father—"

Seth recognized the name at once. "Oh, of course. I heard of your unfortunate loss, Miss Shelby. You have my deepest sympathy. We'll refund the fee he paid right away, if you'll just let me know where to bring it."

"That won't be necessary."

Seth frowned in confusion. "We can't keep—"

She regarded him steadily. "Well, you see, that's why I've come. My sister and I will be leaving with the rest of the group, just as planned. So the registration money our father paid you is rightfully yours."

Red Hanfield choked on the gulp of coffee he had just taken. One side of his mustache hiked upward in a comical expression of uncertainty as he sat back down.

Seth had trouble finding his own voice. Aware that patrons

at the nearby tables were gawking at them, he finally managed to link a few words together. "Surely you're joking, Miss Shelby."

"No, I am quite serious. We will be ready to leave with the other wagons."

Searching for just the right reply, Seth kneaded his jaw, then met her relentless gaze. "Look, miss. I don't mean to be rude, but whatever your intentions were before you came here, you're gonna have to forget them. There's no way we can let you and your sister make the journey. In fact," he reached for the inside pocket of his leather jacket and withdrew a thick packet, from which he pulled out several bank notes. He pressed them into her hand. "Here. This is the cash your father paid for the trip. Take my advice and go back to wherever it is you came from."

He could tell just by looking at her—rooted in that spot without a change in her countenance, other than the obvious set of her teeth—that his words had not dissuaded her one bit.

"I cannot take this," she said flatly. Placing the funds intact on the table beside him, she held her ground. "My sister and I are quite set on this. We will be going west. Good day, Mr. Holloway. Mr. Hanfield." Turning on her heel, she headed for the door.

Seth cast an incredulous look at Red, who made no effort to hide his amusement. Then he snatched up the bank notes and used them to punctuate his words in his friend's face. "Thanks for backing me up, buddy!" With a huff of disgust, he started after Amanda Shelby.

He caught up with her three doors down, in front of the Bluebird Saloon, where raucous piano music from inside the swinging doors tinkled around them, creating an absurd carnival atmosphere for any intended serious conversation. Frowning, he tapped her shoulder.

She stopped and turned, and her eyes flared wider. Instantly, a soft vulnerability in her features disappeared behind a facade of purposeful determination. "Oh, it's you."

"Who'd you expect?" he spat, instantly regretting his harsh tone. "Look, take the—" Conscious of the intense interest of a growing number of passersby, Seth knew better than to wag a handful of cash out in the open, and instead slid the bank notes back within the confines of his jacket pocket. Then he grabbed Amanda Shelby's elbow, ignoring the mortification that glared at him from her narrowed eyes, and steered her to an unoccupied spot a short distance away. There he turned her to face himself. "Please, Miss Shelby. I've been called blunt at times and have probably hurt a few feelings in my day, so if I'm hurting yours I'm sorry. But you don't seem to understand. The journey west is grueling, even for tough, experienced folks, and some of the hardiest souls won't survive it, let alone a couple gals like you and your sister."

"I don't believe that."

"Do you know how to shoot?"

"No, but—"

"Can you change a wheel? The trail rattles the best wagon to shambles."

"No."

"How about repairing harness?"

The last thing he was prepared for was the sheen of tears that glazed her eyes before she lowered them in defeat. It nearly melted his resolve altogether. But she blinked quickly and brushed the imprint of his grip from her dark blue sleeve before raising her gaze to his.

"But. . .we have to go," came her small voice.

There ought to be a law against a gal crying, for what it did to a man inside, Seth thought fleetingly. He hardened himself against the sight of her whisking a stray tear from her cheek as he mustered up all his reason. "Look, if there was some way we could let you come, any way at all, we would. I mean that. But it's out of the question. Even if by some stretch of the imagination you could make the trip—and you can't, take my word for it—at best, you'd slow us down. You're too much of a risk. Now I'm taking you back to your hotel, and when we get there I'm giving you back your father's registration fee. That's my final word on the subject."

Her shoulders sagged in hopelessness, and her despair cinched itself around the middle of Seth's stomach. But he had to hold firm. It was the only thing to do, and all for the best. In time she'd see it, too. He watched her turn and walk mutely toward the Bradford.

Seth accompanied her without speaking. When they reached the hotel, he escorted her inside, then once more pressed the money her father had paid him weeks ago into her palms.

She didn't even look at him.

He cleared his throat. "Again, my deepest sympathy to you and your sister in your loss. I wish you well. Good day, Miss Shelby."

Seth felt like a heel as he strode away from her and called himself every choice name he could think of. But the entire scheme was insane. Any fool could see that. There was no way on earth two very young—not to mention unattached—females could endure the hardships that faced the emigrants on the Oregon Trail. All the overlanders started out with grandiose visions and optimism. . .but the entire route was littered with discarded furniture and household possessions, carcasses of dead horses and oxen, and worse yet, graves of every imaginable size. As if the trek weren't rough enough over rugged mountains and endless blazing prairie and desert, there were plenty enough other threats—wild animals, bizarre weather, Indians, disease—to instill fear in the stoutest heart. It took everything a person had, not to mention an unquenchable, unbeatable spirit to make that journey.

It took a much more valiant heart than Amanda Shelby possessed. . .but that didn't make Seth feel any less like a cowardly snake for being the one to shatter her dreams.

three

Amanda trudged wretchedly up the enclosed staircase to the second floor. Earlier this morning she had managed to acquire at least a portion of peace after kneeling before the Lord in prayer. Now a scant few hours later the grand plans were in ashes. Hopeless. And simply because of that insufferable, overbearing Mr. Holloway with his long, rugged face and squinty eyes and morbid words. How was she going to break the news to Sarah after all their high hopes?

Reaching their room, Amanda drew a deep breath to fortify herself. Why, oh, why had life taken such a sad turn? Why did Pa have to die and leave them stranded way out here so far from everything they knew? Wasn't it heartbreaking enough that death had claimed Mama and the tiny baby her frail body had not been strong enough to bring into the world, without heaven's laying claim to Pa as well? And that, on top of—

No! her mind railed. *You cannot think about him. Not now. Not ever.*

Well, whatever the reasons the little family had been dealt such dreadful blows, Mama would have been the first to remind her girls that God's ways are often beyond understanding, and one should accept troubles just the same as good fortune. But that, Amanda reflected with a sigh, was truly hard to do. She straightened her shoulders and reached for the latch.

Sarah Jane looked up from writing in her journal and sprang to her feet, her face a portrait of bright expectation as Amanda entered the room. "Well? How did your meeting with the wagon master go? Tell me everything!"

"Not as well as we hoped," Amanda fudged. Then seeing

her sister's crestfallen expression, she decided to come right out with the truth. "Mr. Holloway refuses to allow us to accompany the rest of the wagon train."

"You can't mean that!"

She nodded. "He returned the money Pa paid him and practically ordered me—and you—to go *'back where we came from,'* as he put it. I'm really sorry." Untying her bonnet, Amanda slid it off, not caring as it slipped from her fingers to the floor. The urge to give it a swift kick under the bed was hard to resist. . .but it wouldn't solve anything, and someone would only have to retrieve the thing. Instead, she flopped onto the quilted coverlet and lay staring up at the dismal ceiling.

"I don't believe it!"

"Believe it, Sissy. There was no reasoning with that obnoxious, opinionated, bullheaded man. He didn't give me a chance to explain our plight."

"How. . .perfectly horrid!" Sarah declared. "Forbidding people their destiny." With a toss of her golden curls, she flounced over to where she'd been putting her innermost thoughts down on paper and tore the half-written page out of the journal, crumpling it in her hand. An oppressive silence hovered in the room as Sarah plopped grimly back onto the chair, arms crossed in front of her, staring at the opposite wall. Her exhaled breaths came out in a succession of audible exclamation points.

Amanda finally broke the stillness. "Well, this isn't getting us anywhere. I'm going downstairs for the noon meal, and while I eat I'll think about groveling at Mr. Cavanaugh's feet to persuade him to take that wagon off our hands. Much as I hate the prospect, it's the only sensible solution left to us. At least it'll give us money to live on until we make other plans."

Sarah shrugged. "Whatever you say. I'm not hungry. In fact, I may never be hungry again. Think I'll wander on over to the mercantile and browse through the fabrics and jewelry.

It doesn't cost anything just to look. And afterward I may go visit Nancy Thatcher at the bakery until she closes up."

Seated in the dining room moments later, Amanda heard scarcely a word of the cheerful chatter bantered about the rectangular pine table by other hotel guests during the meal. Her thoughts were occupied back at Martha's Eatery, upon the most infuriating man she had ever had the occasion to meet.

Seth Holloway certainly seemed taken up with his own importance, she concluded, swallowing a spoonful of beef stew. Not even allowing her an opportunity to explain the reasoning behind the decision she and Sarah had made. Who did he think he was—ruler of the world? Humph. Some king he would make, in buckskins, with a face that looked in need of a good shave, unruly dark brown hair and hooded, deep-set brown eyes that had a sneaky quality to them. Even that low voice of his rasped in her memory as the conversation mentally took place again. *Go back where you came from.* It would serve the beast right if the sky clouded over and rained for days and days, making the trail impassible for a month. Or better yet, forever. Then he'd have to give everyone's money back, leaving him flat broke.

As she bit into some warm cornbread, a glance out the window revealed the object of her scathing thoughts passing by with his partner and several other men, obviously from the wagon encampment. He wasn't exactly smiling—in fact, Amanda had serious doubts the man ever broke into a smile at all. But he did appear pleasantly cheerful and walked with long, confident strides.

What she wouldn't do to take him down a peg. He had no right to refuse her and Sarah's inclusion with the rest of the overlanders, no right at all. If only she'd become acquainted with some of the migrating families there might have been someone to stand up for them and demand they be permitted to join the company. But when Pa had come down with chills and fever it made folks leery of coming too close, so Amanda had moved the wagon to a spot some distance from the encampment. And after he expired, she and Sarah had mostly kept to themselves in the hotel. It was too late to try to make a friend now. Much too late.

❧

"Mr. Randolph," Seth said, resting a hand on the lantern-faced man's shoulder as he, Red, and two other emigrant leaders walked toward the hardware store, "I'm calling a meeting around the campfire this evening after supper. I want all the men to be present. Think you can handle that?"

The older man stroked his close-cropped beard and gave a nod of agreement. "No problem at all, Mr. Holloway. We're all pretty anxious to leave, after sittin' around for nigh on three weeks."

The heavyset man on the end snorted. "That's an understatement—it's been four weeks for us. It's getting harder and harder to keep a handle on all the loose young'uns. Even the womenfolk are antsy."

"We understand, Mr. Thornton," Red chimed in. "But your waitin's about over, an' now we need to go over the rules we expect folks to abide by for a smooth crossin'."

He nodded. "We'll be there. Count on it."

"Soon as we get back to the wagons we'll spread the word," Randolph said, glancing to the others.

"Good." Seth touched the brim of his hat as they reached the store. "See you then, gentlemen." He turned to Red as the other men entered the establishment. "Guess I'd better start getting my own gear together."

"Me, too. Say, did you manage to smooth that little gal's feathers—about heading west?"

"Fortunately, yes. Took some convincing, though." He shook his head with a droll smirk. "Can't imagine a girl being fool enough to think she—and a sister who I know is even younger than she is—could make a journey like that all by themselves. But at least they're off our hands. I gave their pa's money back. That's the end of it, far as I'm concerned."

❧

Amanda hesitated outside the mercantile for as long as she could, dreading the inevitable. Then, knowing the task would never get any easier, she slipped inside as two chattering women exited. She didn't see Sarah Jane in the store, but spied Mr. Cavanaugh across the cluttered room, chewing on a fat cigar while he spoke with another customer beside the pickle barrel. Amanda stopped near the display of fabrics and fingered a bolt of violet watered silk as she eyed the proprietor with disdain, taking in the waistcoat that strained across his protruding belly, the shiny bald circle atop his head.

His gaze flicked her way and a snide quirk twisted his thick mouth. He excused himself and approached Amanda in self-assured calm. "Well, well. Had a feeling I'd be seeing you sooner or later, Miss Shelby."

She dipped her head slightly. "Mr. Cavanaugh."

"Come to accept my offer, did you?"

"Well, I—"

"Course, I haveta tell you, the stuff's not worth as much to me now, with the train about to leave. I'll have to lower the price some. You understand, I'm sure. I'm still doin' you a favor. Least I can do, under the circumstances."

Amanda stiffened. The man was actually gloating! All so certain that she'd hand over what amounted to the entirety of her and Sarah's worldly possessions for next to nothing! And she had no doubts whatsoever that the moment he got hold of all those supplies he'd take advantage of some other poor souls—turning her misfortune into an indecent profit for himself. She felt her spirit grow ice solid. The sudden reply that popped out of her mouth surprised even her. "I didn't come about the wagon. I'd like to arrange a trade. My father's tools for some dry goods."

"Hm." He rubbed his chin in dubious thought. "I s'pose that could be done—"

"Fine. I'll bring them to you shortly, then, and choose some yardage."

"What about the rest? The outfit. The supplies?"

She offered a cool smile. "We're only discussing Pa's tools, Mr. Cavanaugh. I'm afraid our wagon isn't for sale after all. We do thank you, however, for your. . .*generous* offer. Good day." Gathering a fold of her skirt in one gloved hand, Amanda whirled and fled before she changed her mind.

She fairly flew back to the hotel and up the contained staircase to her rented room. A depressing heaviness settled over her. Her own pride had just caused her to act prematurely— and make a decision that could end up being far more foolish than anything Sarah had ever conceived. What was that verse Pa had quoted so often? "Pride goeth before a fall"? Well, if she and Sarah were in for a big fall now, it would be all her fault.

Letting herself in, Amanda released a shaky breath of relief to discover her sister had not yet returned. At least there'd be time to reason things out, to pray. Instead of coming from the mercantile with cash in hand for the two of them to live on until they decided what to do, she had just thrown their one chance away. She sank to her knees in yet another frantic prayer.

Dear Lord, I've really done it this time. Slammed a door You left standing wide open for us. . .and all because of my silly pride. But Mr. Cavanaugh wasn't being fair to Sarah and me. He just wasn't. You must want us to go west. You must. She paused, rolling her eyes heavenward as if expecting to see the answer inscribed bright and clear on the ceiling. Finding none, she closed her eyes once more. *So we need You to help us now. I know You will see us through.*

Trusting that to be sufficient, Amanda picked up Pa's Bible and took a seat in the overstuffed chair near the window. When her sister's light step sounded outside the door a short time later, she looked up from the Psalms and met the younger girl's curious eyes with a smile.

"I take it you were successful," Sarah Jane said airily. "We have funds to tide us over for a while, until we can find some kind of employment."

"No, I'm afraid not."

"No?" The younger girl removed her shawl and draped it on the nearest chair. "You did go to see Mr. Cavanaugh."

"Yes—" Amanda felt her face growing warm, and looked away. "But I could not let that brute *steal* our things. He wanted to give me less than before. *Less!* Can you imagine? I couldn't bring myself to let him cheat us like that. I just couldn't."

Sarah crossed the room and knelt at her feet, eyes troubled and imploring. "But. . .what will we do now, Mandy, when our money runs out?"

Giving her sister's hand a pat where it rested on her own atop the Bible in her lap, Amanda shrugged nonchalantly. "You said it last night. We're going west, just as we decided."

"But the wagon master said—"

"I know what he said. But I've been thinking about it, and we're going anyway. . .just not with him."

"I don't understand."

"We'll wait until the others have all gone. Then, later on that day or the next, we'll follow behind them. No one will be the wiser."

"Do you think we can do such a thing? Truly?"

"Of course. We belong to the Lord, you and I. God will take care of us. He has to—after all, He promised, didn't He?"

"I. . .suppose."

Amanda forced herself to relax and appear calm and assured. It wouldn't do for Sarah to know how doubtful her older, wiser sister actually felt in the hidden reaches of her heart. Journey across half a continent. Alone.

four

Amanda got barely a wink of sleep all night. One minute she was convinced she'd made the only decision that had any merit, but the next, the absurdity of considering such a monumental undertaking assaulted her. She couldn't even pray. Despite numerous attempts, the words refused to come out right. It seemed folly to expect the Lord to bless their venture, when the wagon master himself pointed out how lacking she and Sarah were in many of the basic and necessary travel skills.

Heaven only knew exactly what they might encounter ahead. Swollen rivers, swift and deep from spring rains, trouble with the wagon, possible injuries to herself or Sarah. And what about wild animals that freely roamed the open country? Or Indians? Amanda's stomach knotted just imagining the two of them alone in the wilderness, no one knowing or caring where they were. But on the other hand, she reminded herself, the Bible did say that God was all-knowing, so nothing would take Him by surprise. The Almighty, in His omnipotent wisdom, had surely known that Pa would pass on to his eternal reward and leave them to fend for themselves. The Lord must have a place for them out west. He would be with them. He would take away all their fears. Grasping that conviction, she closed her heavy eyelids and finally dozed off.

A pair of distant gunshots echoed a few hours later, awakening Amanda with a start. Sarah, next to her in bed, was still breathing in the slow, regular pattern of deep slumber. Amanda, her head aching from the lack of sleep, raised the coverlet and slid out of bed, then padded to the window.

The first pale streaks of dawn were beginning to stain the dark sky in the east. Turning her head in the opposite direction, Amanda spotted the golden lantern glow rising from the conglomeration of wagons amassed in the rocky-outcropped meadow near the spring on the edge of town. Everyone had anxiously awaited those signal shots over several unbearably long weeks. She could imagine the people milling about, hitching teams, readying their wagons. What suppressed excitement there must be, what cheerful chatter, bright hope, and sheer happiness. Last-minute preparations before setting out for a new life.

She heaved a sigh. What she would give to be part of that exhilarated throng about to depart for Oregon.

Brisk morning air ruffled over Amanda's bare arms, and she shivered. Hugging herself, she retreated to the warm sanctuary of the bed while her plan reaffirmed itself. No telling how long it would take that whole wagon train along with the vast herd of cattle and livestock to depart Independence. But once a sufficient span of time passed to allow the emigrants to put some distance between themselves and the town, she and Sarah would leave, too.

That settled, Amanda again relaxed, and her eyes fluttered closed.

"Mandy?"

Sarah's voice seemed fuzzy and far away, but the gentle hand shaking Amanda's shoulder felt very real. She raised her lashes. How could it be this bright already? Only a minute ago it was still dark.

"We'll miss breakfast if we don't hurry."

She bolted upright, noting that her sister was fully dressed. "Oh! I must have overslept! Sorry."

"I left water in the basin for you."

"Thanks." Amanda rose and dashed across the room to wash up. The cool liquid she splashed on her face felt refreshing, and she was surprisingly rested after that last unexpected snatch of sleep. After blotting her hands and face on a towel, she shimmied out of her night shift and into her chemise, then reached for the sturdy burgundy calico dress laid out the evening before.

Sarah moved up behind her and helped with the buttons. "Are we, you know. . .still going?"

Amanda peered over her shoulder. Her sister's brow bore uncharacteristic lines of worry. "Of course. Why wouldn't we?"

"I just wanted to make sure."

"But we'd best not let anyone know. If we so much as let a single word slip, good-intentioned people are sure to stop us. We'll bide our time, wait until we can leave unnoticed."

"Right." Finished with the buttons, Sarah nibbled her bottom lip with unconcealed excitement. "I've packed our things."

"Splendid!" Amanda smiled and sat down to pull on her stockings, then jammed her feet into her hightop shoes and used the buttonhook to fasten them. After some quick strokes with the brush she tied her long hair at the nape of her neck with a black velvet ribbon and stood up. "Do I look presentable?"

Sarah nodded.

"Well, what are we waiting for?" Sputtering into a giggle, she hugged her younger sibling. Arm in arm, they headed downstairs to the dining room, reaching it even as a handful of other patrons were taking their leave.

Mrs. Clark, the middle-aged widow who provided hearty meals at the Bradford Hotel, greeted them as they entered the now-empty room. Her apple-dumpling cheeks rounded with her smile. "We wondered where you two were this morning," she said pleasantly, a hand on her wide hip.

"Everything smells luscious," Amanda said, averting her attention from the gray-haired cook to the long table. She resisted the impulse to offer an explanation for their tardiness.

"You missed all the goin's on," the older woman announced. "The train pulled out first thing this morning."

"Oh, really?" Feigning nonchalance, Amanda exchanged a cursory glance with Sarah. "It certainly seems like a perfect day to begin a journey."

"Yep, that it does. Pity you two couldn't be among them. Well, set yourselves down in one of them clean spots, and I'll bring you some flapjacks and eggs right quick."

The remainder of the morning seemed interminable to Amanda and Sarah as they peered constantly out the window, checking the immense, distant trace of dust stirred up by wagons and cattle. Finally they gathered their belongings and stole down to the livery to tuck their bags unobtrusively into the wagon.

The two of them heaved down the heavy chest containing their father's woodworking equipment and lugged it to Cavanaugh's Mercantile. Amanda had to bite her tongue at the pathetic sum the storekeeper offered for the finely crafted tools, but there was no recourse but to accept. She and Sarah ignored his questions as they casually perused the bolts of material he had on hand and chose several different kinds they thought would prove most useful for their new enterprise.

In mid-afternoon, on the pretense of wanting to get current with all their affairs, Amanda settled their hotel bill, and the girls checked their room one last time to be sure they hadn't forgotten anything. No doubt they'd miss the comfort of that big four-poster soon enough, Amanda surmised. But she eagerly anticipated some solitude after the constant racket of this rowdy frontier town.

"There's no sign of dust above the trail now," Sarah Jane mused, closing the window. "Do you think it's time?"

Amanda subdued the butterflies fluttering about in her stomach and gave a solemn nod. "It's now or never. But first we must say good-bye to Pa. It's only right."

With the emigrant train gone from Independence, the diminished noise level outside seemed all the more apparent in the stillness of the grassy knoll just beyond the simple white church on the far edge of the settlement. Amanda and Sarah treaded softly over the spongy ground.

A soft, fresh breeze whispered among the scattered wooden crosses bearing the names and life years of the dear departed. It gently billowed the girls' skirts as they stood gazing down at the forlorn rectangle of mounded earth beneath which Pa lay awaiting the heavenly trumpet call.

Amanda felt a lump forming in her throat, but swallowed hard and sank to her knees to place a bouquet of wildflowers on the grave. It took every ounce of strength she could muster to force a smile. "Pa, Sarah and I've come to say good-bye now," she said, her voice wavering slightly. She drew a deep breath. "We're setting off for Oregon, just like you planned, so this will be the last time we can visit you. Tell Mama. . .we send our love. Farewell."

Beside her, Sarah Jane sniffed and brushed tears from her cheeks. "We'll keep you and Ma in our hearts. . .until we're all together again. We—we love you. Good-bye. . .for now." After a few moments of silence they met each other's eyes and stood. "We'll have an early supper, then head over to the livery and watch for Mr. Plummer to go have his," Amanda announced.

The blacksmith was busy shoeing one of a pair of work horses when they peeked around the edge of the doorway after their meal. But finally he exited his shop and walked over to Martha's Eatery. The door of the restaurant closed behind him.

"This is it." Amanda led the way around back of the livery, where they sneaked inside. Ever grateful that Pa had made her practice hitching up the mules and driving them, she located the required equipment belonging to them and followed her father's instructions to the letter. Then she went to Mr.

Plummer's makeshift desk and left a packet containing sufficient funds to cover the expenses incurred from boarding and feeding the animals, along with a short note of thanks for his kindness.

Everything finally in readiness, they climbed aboard. Amanda released the brake, clucked her tongue, and slapped the traces against the backs of the mules. The heavy wagon lurched into motion, its huge wheels crunching over the gravelly dirt.

Without Pa, the cumbersome vehicle felt huge. Immense. And the mules seemed less than enthusiastic about having to work after weeks of being penned up and lazy. But Amanda gritted her teeth and held on, steering them around the sheltering grove of trees behind the livery and then guiding them in an arc that would soon intersect the trail to Oregon Territory.

Sarah leaned to peer around the arched canvas top at the busy river port they were leaving behind. "I don't think anyone even noticed us drive off. Oh, this is so exciting, Mandy! We're actually doing it. . .heading west, just like Pa dreamed. I can't wait to start writing about it in my journal. I'm going to put down every single thing that happens along the way!" Gripping the edge of the hard wooden seat, she filled her lungs and smiled, staring into the distance.

A person would have to be blind to miss the sparkle in the younger girl's wondrous blue eyes, Amanda conceded. If it weren't for the sobering knowledge that she herself was now in control of both their destinies, she might have shared some of her sibling's lilting optimism. But right now her hands were full. Returning her attention to the long trail stretching beyond the horizon, she put her full concentration on the hard job ahead.

The road west, impossible to miss, already bore deep ruts from vast hoards of wagons that had made the journey in previous years. Amanda filled her gaze with the absolutely breathtaking landscape all around them. Groves of budding trees dotted the gently rolling ground, itself a wondrous carpet of long, silky grasses. Myriad spring flowers speckled the spring green in a rainbow of glorious hues. Surely in such a delightful season of new life, nothing could spoil their adventure. To make certain, Amanda lofted yet another fervent prayer heavenward, beseeching the Lord to bless and protect them on the journey.

"I wonder when we'll reach Oregon," Sarah mused.

"Papa expected it to take months. But according to that guidebook he purchased back home, it's a fairly pleasant drive, even if it is rather long."

"Why would Mr. Holloway try to scare us off, then?"

At the mention of the wagon master's name, Amanda tightened her lips, forcing aside an exaggerated mental picture of his obnoxious smirk and insinuating eyes. "He's just a pompous beast, is all. But he isn't going to stop us now, Sissy. And neither is anybody else. We are on our way west!"

And Seth Holloway will never even know it.

five

Guiding the team over the gently rolling northwesterly trail that ambled along the Kansas River, Amanda drank in the breathtaking wooded ridges lining either side of the serene valley. Springs and patches of timber interspersed a serene landscape much more vast and open than the familiar dense forests and winding, irregular hills of northeastern Pennsylvania. Already she found the spaciousness refreshing, the immense sky overhead magnificent. "Space to breathe," Pa had called it, and now Amanda knew why. She loved being able to see so far in every direction, and swallowed a pang of sadness that he wasn't there to enjoy it, too.

"I'm getting thirsty," Sarah said, drawing her out of her musings.

"We'll stop at that little grove ahead. It looks like a good place to make camp."

The sun had already sunk beneath the horizon, its slanting rays painting the western sky vibrant rose and violet. Amanda halted the mules, then hopped down and began unhitching them.

"I'll gather wood before it gets too dark," Sarah offered, and bustled off out of sight.

❧

Sarah Jane found an abundance of deadfall among the trees and quickly gathered a generous armful. On her way back to the wagon she saw that Amanda had hobbled the mules and was now freshening up at the riverside. Sarah grabbed a towel. "How far do you suppose we've come?" she asked, joining her sister.

37

Amanda shook excess water from her hands before drying them and her face. "Our late start only gave us a couple hours of travel time. We'd better get up early tomorrow if we ever hope to see Oregon."

After a quick light meal of bread and cheese, they returned to the wagon to dress in their night shifts.

Sarah watched her older sister brushing out her long, auburn hair with the usual regulated strokes, then gave her own curls a few dutiful brushes. "Think I'll write for a little while before I blow out the lantern."

"Just don't be long. We need to be on the road at first light." With a yawn, Amanda slid into her side of the mattress and almost instantly fell asleep.

Sarah retrieved her journal and moved closer to the glow of the lantern.

> *Dear Diary,*
> *Today is the most glorious day of my entire life! Amanda and I set off on our adventure to find our destiny. I thought it would seem a little lonesome, traveling by ourselves, but instead it feels more like we have sprouted wings and are completely free. We can make our own rules, which surely must be one of the most wonderful benefits of all.*
> *You cannot imagine how beautiful this wondrous countryside has been so far. It's as if some grand and heroic knight of old rode through the vast stretches of the land and carved out the most lovely of routes westward, full of sparkling rivers and fragrant spring flowers. Somehow it would not surprise me to discover he is still here, mounted upon his swift steed just beyond our sight as he looks after travelers on this road to Oregon, keeping them always from harm.*

Smiling to herself, Sarah closed the book and hugged it.

Imagine if it were true, and some handsome champion were just around the next bend in the trail, ever watchful of the weary pilgrims on their way to a new life. How wonderful to know there was nothing to fear. As glorious as it was to be free now and on their own, a tiny part of her had felt a little afraid of what lay ahead. But since heading west without Pa had been largely her idea in the first place, she'd squelched those feelings and concentrated on the mild weather and the lovely scenery instead. She leaned over and blew out the lamp, then crawled into bed.

The faraway howl of a wolf pierced the night stillness. Sarah's eyes flew open as a second howl answered from much nearer. Nervously she pulled the blankets over her head and snuggled closer to her sister's slumbering form. But not until the vision of a stalwart man astride a glorious golden horse drifted into her thoughts was she able to relax as she imagined him patrolling the grounds around them. A peacefulness settled upon her, and her eyelids fluttered closed.

Morning arrived all too quickly. When Sarah felt behind her, Amanda's side of the bed was empty. She gathered the topmost blanket around her shoulders and went to peer out of the wagon into the semidarkness.

Amanda was fully clothed and kneeling before a feeble fire she was coaxing to life.

"You're up early," Sarah called. "It's not even light yet."

"Thought we'd better not waste any of this morning if we expect to ever get anywhere."

"Of course. I'll wash up and get dressed."

Her older sister nodded and set a pot of water over the flames to boil. By the time Sarah got back, Amanda was stirring a thick mixture of mush.

"I wonder if it's supposed to be this hard to stir," she commented as Sarah handed her two tin bowls. Then with a shrug she ladled out a sticky gob for each of them, and they took seats on a fallen log. Amanda bowed her head. "We thank you, Heavenly Father, for this new day and for the food you've provided. We ask your blessing and continued presence on our journey. In Jesus' name, amen."

"Amen," Sarah whispered, then smiled. "It smells good." She spooned some of the gooey substance to her mouth, struck by the unusual taste—or lack of same—as she slowly chewed.

Amanda, beside her, spit hers out. "Blah. This is horrid."

"What did you put into it?"

She shrugged. "Just cornmeal, flour, and water."

"Not even salt?"

Amanda shook her head. "I didn't know it needed any. Maddie's mush always tasted just fine."

"I think she used a bit of sugar, too. And maybe it didn't need flour."

"Well, how was I to know?" Amanda huffed.

"Sorry." Sarah bit her lip at her sister's uncharacteristic outburst. "I'm sure if we just sprinkle some salt in it now, it'll help," she said hopefully, and went to get some at the wagon. "Anyway, I'm more thirsty than hungry. That coffee should be about finished, shouldn't it?"

Amanda's glum face brightened. "I'll pour us some." But when Sarah returned with the salt box, an irregular black stain in the dirt steamed next to the fire.

"Thank your lucky stars you didn't even taste it," Amanda said miserably. "We'll just have some water instead." She offered one of the two cups she held.

"I'm not that fond of coffee anyway," Sarah assured her, taking it. "As a rule, I'd much prefer tea." She bent over and sprinkled a pinch of salt into the pot of mush, then reached for the wooden spoon. But the mixture had hardened, and now the spoon stuck fast, right in the middle. It would not even budge. Sarah fought hard to restrain a giggle as Amanda groaned.

"We are going to starve to death, do you realize that?" her sister groused. "This breakfast wasn't even fit for pigs. And look at this pot. The mush is hard as a rock." With a grimace she tossed the container, spoon and all, into the weeds.

"Well, no matter," Sarah said brightly. "We can have more of that two-day-old bread Nancy from the bakery was going to tear up for the birds. And there's lots of cheese in the corn-meal barrel."

While her older sister put the collars on the mules and hitched them to the wagon after the meager breakfast, Sarah traipsed happily from the grove with another armload of dried wood, which she put in back. Then the two of them climbed aboard. Glancing backward shortly after they drove off, Sarah saw a small coyote prance tentatively up to the castaway pot of mush. He put his snout into it, then scampered away. She almost laughed out loud as she settled back onto the seat. It would make a funny entry in her diary, one she'd have to keep secret.

❧

Amanda hoped they would cover a decent stretch of ground before nightfall. So far there had been no trace of the wagon train ahead. She couldn't help wondering how many miles' advantage the emigrants had. But before any thought of Mr. Holloway could intrude, she glanced at Sarah, who was removing some light blue thread and a crochet hook from her sewing bag.

"Thought I'd work on a baby cap," her sister said, nimbly forming the first few loops of a chain stitch.

"Good idea. During our nooning today I'll cut out some aprons. We should be able to work by firelight in the evenings. By the time we reach Oregon we could have a fair number of things made for our store."

Sarah smiled and went on crocheting as they left their first camp behind. Before them lay even grander spring displays amid the trees and swells of the greening landscape, and the cheery songs of bobolinks echoed across the meadows.

The first narrow stretch of the Blue River to be crossed presented no difficulty, and after fording it they stopped for dinner and a rest. Amanda figured it was probably too much to hope the entire trip would pass as smoothly and effortlessly as these first days, but in any case, it was better to dwell in the moment. No sense borrowing trouble.

Another long day of lumbering onward began a set routine as the girls divided chores related to making camp each evening and breaking it the next morning. Good as her word, Sarah took over the cooking, so Amanda no longer dreaded noonings and suppertimes. The throat-closing splendor of green swells star-dusted with tiny frail blossoms and great spillings of mountain pink, larkspur, and other more vivid wildflowers continued to fill them with awe.

"The train must have spent a night here," Amanda stated, hopping down from the wagon one evening. They had stopped near a solitary elm with a trunk three feet thick. The tree towered over the headwaters of a little creek. "There've been lots of cook fires here recently."

Sarah placed a hand on her hip. "Yes, and they didn't leave much wood, you'll notice." Tightening her lips, she walked some distance away to find enough to make supper.

The middle of the following day they passed the fork where the Santa Fe Trail split off in a more southwesterly route, a landmark Amanda regarded in silence, brushing off the solemn reminder she and Sarah were in the middle of nowhere.

❧

"What's that up ahead?" Sarah asked one afternoon, looking up from a flannel baby blanket she was hemming.

"Must be the ferry over the Kansas River." Amanda had been assessing the questionable-looking scows at the edge of the wide, swiftly running water ever since she'd first glimpsed them. And the nearer they came, the less optimistic she felt—especially considering the two somewhat dishevelled, black-haired characters in buckskin breeches and rumpled calico shirts who were manning the contraptions. She would have rather faced another cozy little stream like others they had driven through.

"They're Indians!" Sarah murmured. "Unsavory ones like we saw loitering around Independence. Is this the only spot we can cross?"

Amanda shrugged. "It's part of the trail. The rest of the train must have crossed here."

"Well, I don't like the way those two are snickering and leering at us."

Amanda took note of the more-than-interested glances the swarthy pair aimed at them while muttering comments behind their bony hands. The fine hairs on her arms prickled, and her heartbeat increased. Glancing nervously upstream and down, she saw no fordable sites and wished as never before that they were in the company of other travelers. She swallowed and sent a quick prayer heavenward, pretending a confidence that was far from her true feelings as she drew up to the edge of the steep bank and stopped the team.

"Good day."

One of the unkempt men approached. A lecherous smile curved one end of his mouth. "No more wagons?" Beady dark eyes peered around the schooner, searching the distance before exchanging a wordless look with his chum.

The second one's lips slid into a knowing grin. He stepped nearer, hungrily eyeing Sarah up and down.

Amanda's skin crawled. She barely subdued a blush as Sarah's hand latched onto hers.

The motley louts whispered something. Then, black eyes glinting with devilment, the taller one took hold of the wagon to hoist himself up.

"It's all right, Pa," Amanda said over her shoulder. "We've reached the ferry."

The man paused.

Amanda quelled her sister's questioning expression with a stern look, then returned her attention to the Indians. "He's feeling poorly. Came down with a fever early this morning." The calmness in her voice amazed even her.

"Fever?" Dark fingers instantly released their grip on the wagon. He leapt backward.

The other, with some hesitance, thrust out his palm. "Five dollar for wagon. Two more for mules. One for passengers."

Amanda was fairly sure the price was outrageous, but wasn't about to make an issue of it. She smiled politely and turned to Sarah. "Go inside, Sissy, and get the money from Pa, will you?" As the younger girl complied, Amanda prayed all the more fervently for the Lord's help and protection.

When Sarah returned, Amanda forced herself to remain casual as she placed the fee in the dark hand.

He motioned the two of them inside the rig, and the girls watched out the back while a rope that had been looped around a tree was attached to the wagon. The taller Indian led the team forward toward the boat, while the other used the rope to help slow the schooner's descent down the bank. When everything was finally positioned on the ferry, the men used poles and paddles to propel the scow across the fast current. On the other side, the larger of the dark-skinned pair drove the team through deep sands leading up the northern bank and a short ways beyond. Halting the mules, he nodded to Amanda and jumped off, then loped back to join his cohort on the return across the river.

With the greatest relief, Amanda drew what seemed like her first real breath since the entire process had begun. She emerged from the confines of the wagon bed and moved to the seat.

Sarah, inches behind, grabbed her in a hug. "I'm so glad they believed you. I was never so frightened in my whole life."

"Me neither." Returning the embrace, Amanda gathered her shattered emotions together and allowed herself a moment to stop shaking. Then she clucked her tongue to start the mules and put as many miles between them and the Kansas River as they could before stopping for the night.

After a supper of bacon and fried mush, Sarah refilled their coffee mugs. "I'm too tired to sew tonight," she said on a yawn.

"It's been a long day." Amanda looked dejectedly down at her hands, growing tender from the constant rubbing of the traces against her soft flesh.

"I think there are some of Pa's work gloves in the back," Sarah offered. "They might make the driving easier."

Amanda only stared.

"Or shall I take a turn tomorrow?"

"Actually, that's more what I had in mind, if you must know," Amanda admitted.

"Well, that's fair. You shouldn't have to do it all."

இ

After the nooning stop, Amanda took the reins again, more relaxed after Sarah's turn driving than she would have thought possible. The rhythmic, soothing clopping of the hooves and the jangle of the harness now brought a misty half-consciousness, and she lost herself in memories of their old life, of family times.

Very few people enjoyed such a privileged existence as she and Sarah had once known. But that was before their father's partner—bile rose in Amanda's throat—her own betrothed, had swindled Pa and absconded with all the cash from the land investments, leaving him alone to face creditors and wronged clients. Amanda felt partly responsible for her pa's death, though she had never voiced the dire thought. Morris had fooled them all. Only through her father's grit and hard work, plus the sale of the grand house and most of their worldly possessions, had all the monies been repaid. The three of them were able to set out for Oregon with their heads high.

Even if we would have preferred to stay home, Amanda mused caustically, immediately cutting off thought of the dastardly blackguard whom she had foolishly trusted enough to promise her heart. Well, at least he was out of her life. She was twenty now—old enough to know better than to trust any man's sweet words, ever again. She would remain forever a spinster, one whose sole responsibility in life was to look out for her beautiful younger sister—and she would do that to the very best of her ability. Firm in that resolve, her gaze rose idly into the hazy distance.

A jolt of alarm seized her.

A sullen, angry mass of clouds churned across the faraway horizon.

"Uh-oh. Looks like we might be in for some rain."

Her sister looked up. "Well, a shower shouldn't bother us. The wagon, after all, does have a double-canvas top."

Amanda could only hope the younger girl was right. But eyeing the irregular black cloud bank crawling toward them from the west, she had a niggling fear it was no mere spring shower heading their way.

She urged the team faster as the pleasant breeze began to turn strong and cold.

All too soon the first jagged bolts of lightning forked the slate-gray sky in the distance. Amanda strained to hear the low growl of thunder, then nudged Sarah. "We'd better stop for today. We'll have an early supper."

At the nearest likely spot, they made camp in the fading light, then draped India-rubber tarps over the bedding and the barrels of supplies. Amanda tied the drawstring closure tight on their haven, and the girls wrapped in shawls and sat down in the eerie darkness, hoping the mules would fare all right.

Soon enough, a strong gust of wind rattled the wagon. The arched top shuddered. A mule brayed.

Amanda drew her lips inward as tentative raindrops spattered the canvas. Maybe Sarah was right, it was just a shower after all. But relief vanished almost as quickly as it had come.

The gentle patter turned sinister. With each second, the pounding overhead grew more deafening. The torrent roared over the heavy bowed top, pouring down the sides of the wagon and splashing onto the ground.

A bright flash of lightning glowed through the sodden

fabric like daylight for a split second. An earth-shattering boom of thunder rent the night.

Sarah's scream was drowned out by another blast. Amanda huddled close to her, cringing with every flash and crash. Rain began to drip through the cover overhead, trickling down onto the tarpaulins.

"I'm c-cold," Sarah said, shivering as she inched nearer.

Thunder boomed again.

"This has to end sometime," Amanda assured her as an icy drop spattered her nose and rolled off her chin. She hugged herself and tucked her chin deeper into her shawl, pressing close to her sister.

The elements crashed around them for what seemed like forever. Then, ever so gradually, almost imperceptibly, the thunder began to lessen in degree. The spaces between lightning bolts grew longer. Amanda eased out from under the heavy tarp and went to peer through the closure to see how the trail was faring. She gawked in dismay when a bright flash revealed they were surrounded by a sea of water and mud. The wagon ruts were not even visible.

A small part of her harbored the wish they had the comforting company of the other emigrants, but she was not ready to concede that the know-it-all Mr. Holloway had been right. Surely this wasn't the first bad storm that faced an overlander on the westward trek. If others had made it through, so would she and Sarah Jane.

"If I weren't so cold, I could at least play my guitar," Sarah groused. "It would pass the time."

Amanda silently thanked the Lord for the cold. It was bad enough being soggy and chilled without adding the headache of Sarah's toneless singing. Soon would come the blessedness of sleep, when they would be less aware of how miserable they were. Heaven only knew how long the rain would last. It had to stop sometime. It had to.

six

"Steaming! We're steaming!"

"What?" Amanda opened her eyes, momentarily blinded by bright sunshine. How had they slept so late?

"Look at everything, Mandy," Sarah insisted.

With a yawn and a stretch, Amanda lifted the drenched tarp and sat up. Fragile wisps of mist floated upward in the confining interior of the wagon bed from the scattered tarpaulins and blankets. Rising, she untied the drawstring and leaned out.

The sodden earth sparkled in newly washed glory. Beside them, the rushing stream and a thousand puddles reflected the last puffs of cloud and the blue sky. And Sarah was right. The whole wagon was steaming in the warmth of the brilliant sun. So were the hobbled mules, unharmed and grazing contentedly nearby.

"See if any of that last wood you gathered is still dry," Amanda said. "We'll have hot tea to go with our breakfast. While the water heats, we'll open the sides and set things out to dry."

Sarah stripped down to her drawers and chemise, then rooted through the piles of damp supplies to find the wood she'd wrapped in blankets. "It's not wet at all, Sissy."

Within an hour, the bushes in the surrounding area sported a colorful array of blankets, linens, and articles of clothing, and the soft spring breeze wafted over them while the girls sipped mugs of tea. The temperature warmed considerably, inching higher and higher, the opposite extreme from the previous day.

Alas, the soggy rutted road ahead looked less than hopeful.

The ground remained spongy to the foot, much too soft for travel. Amanda knew they'd be stuck here for at least a couple days, but if nothing else, they'd have ample time to sew.

In the middle of the third lazy afternoon, Sarah laid aside the sunbonnet she'd finished and stretched a kink out of her spine with a sigh. "Know what I'd love right now?"

"What?" Amanda recognized that particular spark in her sister's eyes.

"I would absolutely adore a bath."

"You're kidding, right?"

"Not at all. I'm dying to wash my hair."

"But the stream is still swift and muddy from the rain."

"I know, but we can stay near the edge, can't we? And we can rinse off with rainwater from the barrel. Wouldn't you just love to be clean again—all of you, instead of just washing up?"

"That water was freezing cold when we did our clothes. And besides, we're out in the open."

"So? We haven't seen a living soul since we crossed the river on the ferry. And anyway, we can leave our drawers on."

Amanda searched all around and beyond, as far as she could see. There truly wasn't anyone in sight. For all intent and purpose, they were the only two people in this part of the world. And she had to admit, she did feel grubby. What harm would there be in taking a quick dip, so long as they stayed in shallow water? "Well, I suppose we could try it."

"Oh, good!" Sarah all but tore out of her shirtwaist and skirt and undid her hair ribbon. Grabbing a cake of rose-scented soap and a towel, she dashed, shrieking, into the rushing water.

Amanda, not far behind, gasped when she stepped into the frigid flow. This was going to be the quickest bath in history. But once she was completely wet, the water didn't seem quite so cold, and the sunshine blazing down on them felt incredibly warm. A sudden splash drenched her.

Sarah giggled.

Turning, Amanda met her sister's playful grin. "So that's how it's going to be, eh?" Leaning down, she skimmed the surface of the water with her palm, directing an arc of water at the younger girl. It cascaded down her face, and over her shoulders.

"Enough, enough! I'm sorry!" Hand upraised in a gesture of defeat, Sarah acquiesced and began wetting her hair.

Amanda followed suit. But seeing her sister bent over at the waist with her behind in the air as she rinsed her long hair was too much to resist.

A little shove, and in Sarah went, headfirst. She came up sputtering, ready to reciprocate.

Instead, she froze, eyes wide.

Amanda whirled.

In the distance, a small band of Indian braves on ponies rode straight for them.

Her mouth went dry. "Back to the wagon! Hurry!" Though what security the two of them would find there, she could only question.

After they clambered up into the back, they seized blankets and wrapped themselves up, then perched fearfully on the seat.

Any remaining doubts Amanda may have had regarding the lunacy of this westward venture now vanished. Everyone knew the sad fate that had met Narcissa Whitman and her doctor husband Marcus last November. Missionaries to the Cayuse Indians of the Far Northwest, they had been brutally massacred in their mission home by the very tribe with whom they had labored faithfully for several years.

Now Amanda's dreadful realization that she and her younger sister would soon join Ma and Pa in the hereafter dropped with a thud. She prayed the end would be swift, if not merciful. *Please, Lord, help us to be brave.*

Sarah Jane's expression was no less fearful, but she hiked

her chin. "Well, if I'm about to die, I at least want to go happy." She darted into the wagon bed and returned with her guitar.

Mouth agape, Amanda could not respond.

The Indians were almost upon them now. Their skulls were shaved but for a thick strip of dark hair running from front to back that was roached into an upstanding comb. Naked, except for aprons worn about their loins, they also sported vermillion face paint applied in lurid rings about their eyes.

As if completely oblivious to the approaching uninvited audience, Sarah Jane strummed a few chords of introduction, then sang at the top of her lungs:

> "Oh, don't you remember sweet Betsy from Pike,
> Who crossed the wide prairies with her lover Ike,
> With two yoke of cattle and one spotted hog,
> A tall shanghai rooster, and an old yaller dog?"

> "Sing too-ral-i, oo-ral-i, oo-ral-i-ay,
> Sing too-ral-i, oo-ral-i, oo-ral-i-ay."

> "They swam the wide rivers and crossed the tall
>   peaks,
> And camped on the prairie for weeks upon weeks. . ."

The young braves reined in their pinto ponies and sat motionless atop them, staring dumbfounded as Sarah completely destroyed the tune of the comical song.

Amanda didn't know whether to laugh or cry as her sister continued belting out verse upon endless verse:

> "They soon reached the desert, where Betsy gave out,
> And down in the sand she lay rolling about;
> While he in great terror looked on in surprise,
> Saying, Betsy, get up, you'll get sand in your eyes."

"Sing too-ral-i, oo-ral-i, oo-ral-i-ay,
Sing too-ral-i, oo-ral-i, oo-ral-i-ay."

Still moving nothing but their dark eyes, the Indians passed curiously astonished looks among themselves. They maintained a safe distance as Sarah launched into another four stanzas.

". . .Long Ike and sweet Betsy got married of course,
But Ike, getting jealous, obtained a divorce;
And Betsy, well satisfied, said with a shout,
Good-bye, you big lummox, I'm glad you backed out."

"Sing too-ral-i, oo-ral-i, oo-ral-i-ay. . ."

Amanda, not entirely recognizing some of the ridiculous lyrics, wondered inanely if her younger sibling had penned some of them herself. She was almost relieved when the final phrase ended. Moments of heavy silence ensued. Even the Indian ponies stood as if frozen, except for the occasional flick of a tail.

Amanda had to force herself to replenish her lungs.

"I suppose I should sing a hymn, too, as my last song." Sarah Jane drew a fortifying breath:

"I'm just a poor wayfaring stranger,
While trav'ling through this world of woe,
Yet there's no sickness, toil or danger
In that bright world to which I go."

"I'm going home to see my father,
I'm going there no more to roam,

I'm only going over Jordan,
I'm only going over home."

"I know dark clouds will gather 'round me,
I know my way is rough and steep.
Yet beauteous fields lie just before me,
Where God's redeemed their vigils keep. . ."

As the last note of the fifth stanza died away, Sarah moistened her lips and stood the guitar in the wagon bed, then bravely raised her chin.

Amanda herself had yet to move. She could feel her heart throbbing, her pulse pounding in her ears. Now, awaiting her own most certain demise, she could only wonder what form of torture the two of them faced. How sad that someone so young and pretty as Sarah would meet such a tragic fate, would never find the dashing husband she dreamed of most of her life. If only Amanda could wake up and find this whole foolish idea had been only a dream. Independence could probably have used some good seamstresses. . .there were far worse places for the two of them to live.

After an eternal moment, the brave in the center gave an almost imperceptible signal, and en masse, the band turned their mounts and galloped away. Without even looking back, they crested the top of a near rise and vanished from sight. "D-do you think they'll come back, Mandy?" Sarah asked in a small voice.

Amanda, as befuddled as her sister, merely shrugged.

A ridiculous phrase of off-key singing burst from behind the hill. Then a howl of laughter.

Sarah loosened her soggy blanket and stood. "Humph. They don't even know good music when they hear it!"

At this, Amanda, too, exploded into a giggle, then laughed hysterically until tears coursed down her cheeks. Though her sister joined halfheartedly, it was easy to see she didn't quite see the humor of the moment. Amanda suddenly realized the Indians had thought her sibling was possessed by some strange spirit. . .one they were hesitant to anger. It made her laugh all the harder.

Finally regaining control of her shattered nerves, she turned to Sarah. "Well, Sissy, we can thank the Good Lord for His protection this day. We could easily have made our entrance through the pearly gates."

Sarah paused in the process of stripping off her wet underthings. "I suppose you're right. God definitely is looking after us." But she leaned out, peering in the direction the Indians had taken, just to be sure.

seven

"How's it look up ahead?" Seth asked, riding alongside Red's chestnut gelding in the late afternoon.

"Well, coulda been worse." His friend's copper mustache spread with his grin. "I'd say we've wasted time aplenty. Cy an' T. J. scouted far as the river, an' say the Big Blue's still pretty high from the rain. Trail's hardening up, though. Reckon the worst of the storm passed behind us."

Seth nodded. "Yep, but we have other things to consider, pal. While I was collecting some strays, a bit ago, I spotted a handful of Kanza braves in the distance. Before they get ideas about helping themselves to the livestock, we need to double the guards till we move out of here tomorrow. Pass the word."

"Right, boss."

With a dry smile at his partner's lighthearted formality, Seth waved and headed back toward the rear of the wagon train. The heavy rainfall had necessitated a few precious days' wait for the ground to firm up again, but as Red declared, things could have been worse. Nevertheless, it was the Big Blue they had to worry about most. Always a crotchety river even at the best of times, when it was flowing high, the current was incredibly strong and swift.

Skirting a cluster of cows grazing directly in his path, Seth navigated around them and rode to the crest of the knoll. He took out his spyglass and peered toward the rise where he'd glimpsed the Indians. There was no sign of them at the moment, but no telling where they'd gotten to. He moved the glass and searched what he could see of the undulating landscape.

Just as he was about to inhale a breath of relief, the telescope picked up some movement. He blinked and looked again. No. It couldn't be. He'd counted all the wagons on his way to talk to Red. How could there be a straggler? And several miles behind them, yet! He reined in for a better view.

His heart sank at the sight of two very feminine forms in skirts and bonnets fussing about the winding, silvery ribbon that made up a narrow section of the stream. He had a very strong inclination exactly who'd be fool enough to travel alone in this sometimes-hostile country. "Of all the harebrained—"

Seth took off his hat and rubbed his forehead on his sleeve before replacing it. Another look confirmed his worst fears, and angrily he slumped back into the saddle. It would serve that empty-headed female right if he simply let her and her sister keep on the way they were until they came face to face with that cantankerous river—see what they'd do about crossing those treacherous waters without a ferry. They'd discover soon enough how idiotic they were to set out by themselves. If they had a lick of sense they'd turn around now and return to Independence. Maybe the next train out would take them under supervision, but he wanted nothing to do with them.

Red would never believe this. In fact, Seth had half a mind not to even mention the Shelby sisters to his partner. The last thing the company needed was to be slowed down by two girls who didn't have the sense the Almighty gave a fencepost.

But even as he enumerated in his mind the reasons why he should continue on as if he hadn't seen them, the possibility that those wandering Indian braves might find them easy pickings cut across his resolve. A full train wasn't likely to be attacked, but a single wagon out in the open with two vulnerable young women aboard might be another story entirely. No telling what gruesome fate would befall the Shelby girls then.

Seth realized that the next train that happened along would blame him for whatever misfortune befell the pair and spread the word that he couldn't look out for folks under his care. He'd never lost a family to Indians yet. Cholera and dysentery, yes, accidents and drownings. But even when the odd wagon rumbled apart on the rough trail, he'd always managed to find folks willing to lend a hand to the unfortunates. Emulating his idol, the famous trail guide Thomas Fitzpatrick, Seth was trying to earn a reputation for taking people all the way to their destination—and he wasn't about to let all his hard work be ruined by the likes of Amanda Shelby.

That decided, he ground his teeth and nudged his dapple-gray mount, Sagebrush, into a canter. He'd try one more lecture first, and in the unlikely event Miss Shelby still wouldn't take his advice, he'd figure out what to do then.

&

Amanda washed up the dishes from their early supper of the usual beans and biscuits while Sarah retired to the wagon to record the events of the day in her journal. Tomorrow they would leave this restful campsite. Ahead, miles of rolling prairie in all its green glory stretched to the sky.

This had been their most pleasant stay so far, and restful, thanks to the torrential rain that had brought the journey to a halt. Of course, there had been the encounter with those half-naked Indian braves. Amanda would thank the Lord till her dying day that He'd kept them from harm. She still had qualms regarding further unknown dangers. But as long as the land remained so open, with its gently rolling hills and long prairie grasses, she and Sarah would fare well enough. Amanda couldn't help wondering, though, what lay beyond the horizon.

Standing to shake the excess water off the plates, she lifted her gaze far away to the west, then frowned. It had to be her imagination, the lone rider like a speck of black against the ocean of undulating green. And coming this way! A tingle of alarm skittered up her spine. Is this what they'd be facing every livelong day of this journey? Strange men everywhere they turned? Tomorrow when they stopped for their noon meal, she would get out Pa's rifle and figure out how to use it. Amanda had seen him load and fire it often enough. Surely it couldn't be so hard to master. After all, with Sarah being as fetching and winsome as she was, there might be dozens of occasions when some overly interested man might need to be convinced he should be on his way.

That decided, she sloshed the heavy frying pan in the stream and then wiped it dry while she prayed again for protection. *What time I am afraid, I will trust in Thee.* The precious promise her parents had often quoted drifted to mind, bringing with it the assurance that God was still in control. An unexplainable calm began to soothe her jangled nerves. The cookery and utensils had been stowed away and the campfire doused by the time the rider was near enough for the horse's hoofbeats to be heard. The man looked vaguely familiar, which struck Amanda as curious, since they had gotten to know only a few people during their stay at the hotel. But when he pushed back the brim of his dark hat, revealing his long-faced scowl, her heart sank. The wagon master! For an instant she entertained thoughts of trying to hide, but it was too late. She inhaled a deep breath and assumed an air of indifference as he rode up.

"What do you think you are doing?" he demanded.

Amanda, sitting on a crate, placed the apron she'd been stitching on her lap and looked up. "And good day to you, Mr. Holloway," she returned sarcastically.

"You heard me." The wagon master's brown eyes sizzled with fury as he glared at her from atop his mount, his granite expression hard and rigid as his posture.

"Why, I believe it's quite evident to anyone who can see."

"Yes, well, this has gone far enough. Turn this rig around tomorrow. Won't take you any longer to get back to town than it did to get this far."

Amanda smiled thinly. "Thank you. That's quite the brilliant deduction." She rose casually and started toward the wagon to put her sewing away.

Leather creaked as he shifted position in the saddle. "So

you do have some sense after all."

"I beg your pardon?" She paused and turned, arching her brows.

"You're finally giving up on this brainless notion of yours to head west."

Brainless! Amanda felt growing rage at the crass remark. Only her good breeding enabled her to restrain her tongue as she stared without blinking at the domineering, cantankerous man. "Not at all. My sister and I are getting along just fine. . . not that it's any concern of yours, I might add."

"Is everything all right, Sissy?" Sarah Jane called, leaning to peer from the confines of the wagon.

"Perfectly. Mr. Holloway came to wish us well. And now he's leaving."

"In a dog's age I am," he bellowed. "Now, see here—"

"Really, sir, whatever your purpose in forsaking your own duties to come here, you've said your piece. However, it does not change anything. So I would like you to. . .how did you put it? *'Go back where you came from,'* wasn't it?"

A muscle worked in his jaw. He dismounted and reached to grab Amanda's arm, but she shied away. He rolled his eyes. "Look, Miss Shelby," he began, his patronizing tone an obvious ploy to get her to listen. "I know I sounded a mite blunt when I first rode in. I apologize. It was no way to speak to a lady. But I can't seem to get through to you what you need to hear."

"Oh? And what might that be?" She crossed her arms in supreme disinterest.

He filled his lungs and let the breath out all at once. When he spoke, his voice was much kinder, almost pleasant. "I must admit, I was surprised when I looked back and saw you coming. I wouldn't have thought you'd make it this far."

Amanda, with an inward smile of satisfaction, had to remind herself not to gloat.

"But I have to tell you," he went on, his voice taking on a

more ominous quality. "This is the easy part. When folks start out for Oregon they think the whole trail's gonna be like this. But it's not. Far from it. There's hardship coming up. Real hardship. First off, there's a mighty river just ahead. It's running high and fast now from that rain, and there's no ferry to make the crossing easy. We'll have to float every wagon over it and hope none of them gets swept away in the current. After that will come the mountains. There'll be places so steep we'll have to haul the wagons up one at a time with ropes and chains, then let them down on the other side. Course, a whole passel of them'll rattle apart long before they ever make it that far. And don't forget the watering holes we'll come to that aren't fit to drink. Folks and animals weak with thirst will drink anyway. And every one of them will get sick and die."

Amanda tapped her foot impatiently. Anything to keep from revealing that his dire predictions were beginning to get through to her.

"And that doesn't even take Indians into consideration," he continued. "Or the rattlesnakes, the cholera, and even the weather. You may think you've seen wind and lightning since that little storm we just had. But that was a spring shower compared to what we'll face once we hit the high country. We could get pounded with hail. It could even snow on us before we're through the passes, and the lot of us could freeze to death. Think about it. You've got a younger sister to be responsible for. Is that how you want her to end up?"

Amanda swallowed hard. What he was telling her was the complete opposite of what Pa had read in the guidebook he'd bought. Yet something in the wagon master's face seemed honest. Trustworthy. He'd been over this route before, and he should know more than the books reported. But still— "Well, the Lord has been with Sarah and me up till now, and the Bible says He'll take care of His own always," she reasoned.

Mr. Holloway's demeanor hardened. "I'd say that's a mite presumptuous, myself. Expecting Almighty God to come to your rescue when you don't use the sense He gave you."

Amanda broke eye contact and lowered her gaze to the gritty ground. She took a few steps away, thinking over his words. If she hadn't been enduring the railings of her own conscience along that same line, she'd have been livid. She could not deny that the Lord had already spared them from impending doom twice—and they'd barely begun the journey. Perhaps this was the last chance He was giving them to turn around.

But to what? an inner voice harped.

She stopped and turned. "I want to thank you for coming, Mr. Holloway. I know you mean well. But I'm afraid Sarah and I have to keep going west. We don't have anyplace else to go. If we die along the way, then it's God's will. But we're still going to try."

He slowly shook his head.

"We don't expect you to understand or to feel concern over us. You gave Pa's money back, and we don't have the right to count on you to look after us. We'll just keep on by ourselves. We'll be all right. Now, I'm sure your duties are calling you back to the train. I wish you good day."

He didn't respond for several moments, just stared. Then his expression flattened, along with his tone. "Well, now, that's where we differ. About the last thing I can do is leave the two of you here alone." He hesitated again, a look of resignation settling over his sun-bronzed features. "The train will camp by Alcove Spring tonight so we can start getting everyone across the Big Blue tomorrow. Pack up in the morning and come join up. Travel with the company."

"But—"

"Do it." Without further comment, he swung up into his saddle and galloped away.

Amanda wanted more than anything to ignore Seth Holloway. But for some unexplainable reason, she could not will herself to do so. Nor could she restrain her eyes from gazing after him.

eight

"He's quite handsome, don't you think?" Sarah asked, emerging from the wagon to lounge on the seat, her journal in hand. "In an outdoors sort of way, I mean."

"Hm?" Dragging her gaze from the departing horseman, Amanda turned.

"The wagon master. He's handsome, I said. Not at all the way I pictured him from things you told me."

Amanda barely suppressed a smirk.

"Well, not that he appeals to me, of course," Sarah amended. "I fully intend to find someone much more refined, myself. But in general, Mr. Holloway seems to have a certain. . .charm."

Charm! Amanda thought incredulously. *That's the last attribute I'd assign to Seth Holloway.* "I didn't pay him that much mind," she finally said.

Sarah gave a dreamy sigh. "The man I'm looking for must be head and shoulders taller than anyone I've ever met, and stronger, with gorgeous thick hair, expressive eyes and lips, and a voice that sings across the strings of my heart. And he'll be rich, of course. I refuse to settle for less."

The raspy voice alone would eliminate Mr. Holloway, Amanda decided, but didn't bother answering. After all, his eyes were too dark to be very expressive anyway, and his lips had yet to reflect anything but his anger and irritation. She wondered absently if he ever bothered to smile.

"Are we going to do what he asked?"

"You mean *ordered,* don't you?"

"Well, are we?"

Amanda met her sister's questioning face as Mr. Holloway's

blunt accusation about presuming upon God came to mind. Loath as she was to admit it, his remark did have merit. "Well, at—at first I didn't plan to," she hedged, "but already in the few days we've been on the trail, God has had to rescue us twice. We really shouldn't expect Him to come to our aid every time we encounter any sort of peril."

Sarah did not respond.

"The fact is," Amanda went on, "the wagon master is right. Sooner or later we're going to face some serious difficulties we won't be able to handle on our own. With the other emigrants there'd be someone who could help us. Folks look out for each other. I'm afraid if we don't join the train it could be to our folly."

"I see what you mean." Sarah glanced westward momentarily, in the direction their visitor had taken. Then she sat, opened her diary and began writing once more, a fanciful smile curving her lips.

Amanda saw that Seth Holloway was no longer within sight. Reaching into the wagon, she retrieved her sewing and returned to the crate she'd occupied earlier. If the man had not appeared at their campsite out of the blue, she'd never have guessed the other wagons were within such close proximity. They, too, must have had to wait out the horrific rain. Oh, well, she concluded, knotting the last stitches in the apron she'd been making, if she and Sarah were actually hoping to meet up with them in the near future, it would be wise to turn in soon so they could get an early start. She bit off the remaining thread. After making swift work of attending to all the evening chores, Amanda hurried to the wagon, where she discovered Sarah already asleep in bed. She shed her cotton dress and tugged on her night shift, then took her place beside the younger girl on the hard mattress. But her mind remained far too active to relinquish consciousness easily. In the stillness broken only by the uneven cadence of the night creatures, she analyzed Mr. Holloway's unexpected visit.

Something about the man disturbed her in a way she had never experienced before. It wasn't so much his domineering manner, or even his patronizing attitude toward her and her sister—those she could understand. But when he'd realized they were determined to make the trip with or without the benefit of company, he'd mellowed. For a few seconds he'd even seemed. . .kind. And she preferred him the other way. Sarah was right. Seth Holloway did possess a certain rugged, outdoors look that some might consider handsome. But aware that the man had proclaimed her brainless and foolhardy, Amanda saw no reason to concern herself with such inane fantasies as trying to convince him otherwise. With a sigh, she fluffed her pillow and settled down on its plumpness.

❧

Seth, on the last watch of the night, poured the dregs of the coffee into his mug, then drank it slowly as he walked the outside perimeter of the circled wagons. Spying Red keeping a lookout on the westward side, he joined him. "All's quiet, eh?"

His friend nodded. "Ain't seen hide nor hair of them Injuns or any other creatures lurkin' about."

"Me neither." Seth tossed the dregs from the mug into the bushes. He would have preferred not to have had an encounter with the Shelbys, much less have to talk about it, but it needed to be aired. His partner would also be affected by their joining up with the train. He cleared his throat. "There's something I might as well tell you."

Red looked up, his brow furrowed. "You happened on some other trouble?"

Seth shrugged. "Not exactly. Well, maybe. I, uh, spotted the Shelby sisters trailing us some ways back."

"What?" His partner's jaw went slack, his expression tinged with a combination of humor and disbelief.

"You got it. Fool females took it upon themselves to set out after us. I tried to persuade them to turn around while they still could, but it was no good. Trying to get through to that older one's like butting up against a stone wall." He grimaced and shook his head. "Stubbornest gal I ever did come across."

"Hm. Worse than that sister-in-law of yours is, eh? The one who soured you on marriage, I mean."

Seth didn't dignify the comment with anything but a glower. The mere thought of his younger brother being linked up with that conniving, sharp-tongued Eliza always made him angry. Red snickered, then rubbed his jaw in thought. "Well, if they made it this far on their own, I s'pose they have as much a shot at goin' west as anybody else."

"Maybe. At least on the easy end of things," Seth grated. "Figure if we're gonna end up playing nursemaid, we might as well have them within reach. I told them to join up with us this evening. Who knows, they might get their fill when they stare the Big Blue in the face."

Neither spoke for several seconds.

"Guess I'll head on back to my end," Seth said with resignation. "Folks'll soon be up and cooking breakfast before those cockamamie Sunday services they insist on having."

"Strange comment, if you don't mind me sayin' so— 'specially comin' from the grandson of a circuit-ridin' preacher."

Seth branded him with a glare. "See you later."

"Sure. Could be an interestin' day."

Ignoring his partner's chuckle, Seth strode away.

❧

When Amanda came within sight of the train of emigrants, the next evening, the first thing she noticed was the warm glow of lantern light that crowned the circle of wagons like a halo. It bolstered her spirits, as did the happy music drifting from the encampment from fiddles and harmonicas. Drawing nearer, Amanda heard soft laughter and the sound of children and barking dogs.

"I think I'm going to like being with the others," Sarah said happily.

Before Amanda could answer, her eyes locked on to Seth

Holloway's where he leaned against the nearest rig with his hands in his pockets as if waiting for the two of them to arrive.

His expression unreadable, he shoved his hands into his pockets and walked toward them. "Pull up over there," he instructed with a slight jerk of his head.

Amanda nodded, guiding the team to an empty space in the formation. As she did so, a threesome of men approached. "Evenin', ladies," a solid-chested older man said, thumbing his hat. "Name's Randolph. Nelson Randolph. This here's Ben Martin and Zeke Sparks," he said, tipping his head to the left and right to indicate a rawboned man in his early thirties and a narrow-faced one with a long nose and prominent ears. "We'll help get you into place."

"Why, thank you." Amanda accepted his proffered hand as she climbed down. "I'm Amanda Shelby."

"And I'm Sarah, her sister."

"Glad to make your acquaintance," Mr. Randolph said, reaching to help Sarah also. "We'll be neighbors of yours along the way, so you'll soon get to know us an' some of the others in this mob."

"An' which ones ya should keep an eye out for," Ben Martin said with a good-natured wink. He nudged his lanky pal in the ribs.

In a matter of moments the mules had been unhitched and the wagon rolled into the open slot, its tongue beneath the back of the wagon ahead of it.

"When you gals get settled in," Mr. Randolph said, "make yourselves to home. Mosey in by the big fire and introduce yourselves, if you want to. Folks generally do most of their visitin' in camp. Or just sit an' listen to the music, if you druther. With it bein' Sunday, folks seem to like hymns best."

Amanda smiled. "We'll do that. Thanks for your help."

As the men left, she glanced around self-consciously at the several curious but friendly faces turned their way and returned a few smiles. No one was familiar, but then Amanda hadn't actually met more than one or two emigrants back in Independence before Pa had taken sick. The only person to whom she'd spoken was Mr. Holloway, and he was nowhere to be seen. "Well," she said turning to Sarah, "we're here."

"Yes." The younger girl's gaze swept across the open circle, where a few couples were blending their voices in song. Clusters of children frolicked everywhere.

Amanda recognized her sister's peculiar smile and its accompanying blush immediately. Habitually checking to see which young man in particular had caught Sarah's eye, she noticed a gangly youth who extracted himself from a group of others and sauntered toward them.

"Evening, ladies," he said, grinning broadly on his approach. He doffed his hat in an elaborate gesture, revealing curly brown hair, then plunked it back on, blue eyes sparkling as his attention settled on Sarah. "I'm Alvin Rivers. Delighted to welcome you to camp."

Amanda noted the young man's clothing seemed of finer cut and quality than that of the men they'd met earlier.

"Why, thank you, Mr. Rivers," Sarah gushed. "My name is Sarah Shelby, and this is my older sister, Amanda."

Amanda cringed.

Alvin gave her a respectful nod, then switched back to Sarah again. "Anything I might do to help you get settled in for the night? Check your wheels? Grease the hubs?"

"Grease the hubs?" the younger girl echoed in puzzlement.

"Right. We do it most every night, miss. With the bucket of grease hanging back by the axle."

Both girls followed his gesture.

Amanda hadn't missed his surprise at Sarah's question. She had a vague recollection of Pa mentioning something about that chore, but she'd neglected to do anything about it up until now. How fortunate that Mr. Holloway wasn't around to witness her stupidity. "Thank you, Mr. Rivers," she said. "Sarah and I would be most grateful to have you tend to greasing the hubs this evening." *While I watch to see how it's done!*

"Glad to, miss." He tipped his hat and started toward the back of the wagon, with them in his wake. "Where do you two hail from?" he asked casually over his shoulder.

"Pennsylvania," Sarah answered. "Tunkhannock. And you?"

"Baltimore, Maryland. My aunt and uncle are looking to buy some prime land in the Oregon Territory where there's room to spread out. Too many people were bottled up in the little valley we lived in back east." He took down the grease bucket and set to work.

"Excuse me, miss," Amanda heard someone say. She turned to see a pleasant-faced grandmotherly woman smiling at her, accenting deep laugh creases on either side of her smile. "Since it's late, and all, I thought you and your sister might like some stew. We've finished up, but there's plenty left in the pot. Name's Minnie Randolph. Husband and me are three wagons down." She pointed in that direction.

"Why, thank you, Mrs. Randolph. You're most kind. I'm Amanda, and she's Sarah. Shelby."

"Glad to know you. When we heard you two were coming, I figured you'd be tired by the time you got here. And don't worry about a thing, you hear? A lot of folks're gonna be keeping an eye out for you gals on this trip. We didn't get to know your pa, but he seemed a decent sort the little time we saw him readyin' for the journey. Downright shame he had to pass on so suddenlike." Obviously noting the distress the reminder had caused, she quickly cleared her throat. "You just come right on down as soon as you're ready."

Amanda nodded her thanks. She turned back to Sarah, catching the end of something Alvin Rivers was saying as he finished the last wheel.

". . .so you wouldn't mind if I come by of an evening and show you around?" His voice cracked on the last word.

"That would be very nice," Sarah answered.

And once all the other eligible young men in the group

catch a glimpse of my fair and lissome sister, you'll have to stand in line, Amanda couldn't help thinking.

"Sarah," she called. "We've been offered some supper. Let's go wash up."

Her sister gave a nod of assent, then turned to Alvin. "Thanks for helping out with the wagon. Perhaps I'll see you tomorrow."

"Yes, miss," he said, hanging the bucket back on its hook. He took a large kerchief from a back pocket and wiped his hands. "Tomorrow." The grin he flashed at her broadened to include Amanda. "Miss Shelby."

Amanda nodded. She bit back a giggle as he moved backward, almost stumbling over a rock in his path before he turned and strode away. Then, aware of someone else's scrutiny, she glanced curiously around. Part of her expected to find Seth Holloway's critical gaze fixed on her, ready to find fault, but it wasn't the wagon master after all.

Two wagons ahead, a tall, somber man stared unabashedly. He held a fussing little girl in his arms. Another small child, a boy a year or so older, clung to his knees. He patted the towhead and said something Amanda couldn't hear, then bent and scooped him up. He placed the two tots inside his wagon and climbed in after them.

"I'm ready," Sarah Jane said, coming to her side.

"Hm? Oh. I'll be just a minute." Accepting the dampened cloth her sister held out, Amanda scrubbed her own face and hands, then brushed her hair and retied the ribbon. "Best we not keep Mrs. Randolph waiting." Shaking some trail dirt from the hem of her skirt, she fluffed it out again, and the two went to join the kind older woman.

After enduring even those few days of their own inadequate cooking, their neighbor's hearty stew tasted like a feast fit for royalty. Amanda relished every drop, mopping the last speck from her bowl with the light biscuits, even as steady, sad crying carried from the next wagon. It caught at her heart.

"Would you like more?" the gray-haired woman asked, interrupting Amanda's musings.

"Oh, no, we've had plenty, thank you." Amanda placed a hand on the older woman's forearm. "It was truly delicious."

"I'm afraid we don't share your gift for cooking," Sarah confessed. "All I've managed so far is some pretty ordinary beans with biscuits or cornbread."

"Well, cookin's more skill than gift, I'd say. There'll be plenty of time on this trip for both of you to pick up some of the basics of makin' meals on the trail. I'd be more'n happy to pass on what I know at some of the noonings and suppertimes."

"Why, that's very kind of you." Amanda fought sudden and unexpected tears at the woman's generosity. Up until this past sad year, she hadn't been one given to displaying her emotions, and she sincerely hoped this was not becoming a habit. She must merely be overly tired. She smiled and got up. "We'll just wash up our dishes and bring them back." She nodded at Sarah, and the two hurried to the spring with the soiled things.

The beauty of Alcove Spring was not lost on either one. They gazed in rapt delight at the pure, cold water that gushed from a ledge of rocks and cascaded ten feet down into a basin. Quickly finished with their chore, they left the idyllic spot.

Mrs. Randolph graciously inclined her bonneted head on their return. "I know this has been a long day, so I won't keep you. Tomorrow I'll introduce you to some of the folks around. Meanwhile, don't waste time worryin' about anything. We'll all take real good care of you two."

A wave of reassurance washed over Amanda, and she couldn't help wondering if everyone in the train would be so kind and thoughtful. She lifted a hand in parting and took her leave. "Thanks again. Good evening."

Passing the next wagon, Amanda once more met the brooding eyes of the lanky man sitting inside as he cuddled his two forlorn children. She gave a polite nod and continued on. Tomorrow she'd ask Mrs. Randolph about those little ones.

nine

At the wakeup signal the next morning, the girls expectantly threw on their clothes. From all around the camp, a curious assortment of whistles, snorts, shouts, and cracks of bull-whackers' whips filled the air as the company came to life. Women put coffee on to boil and started the bacon to sizzle over crackling fires, while the men went to gather their oxen or mules and hitch them up. Sleepy-eyed children yawned and stretched, then hustled to wash, dress, and tend to chores before the order came for the wagons to roll.

"Sure is a busy place," Sarah commented, measuring tea leaves into the tin coffeepot.

Amanda only nodded. "I'd best round up the mules while you see to that. We'll have to do like everyone else now." She stepped over the wagon tongue and hurried toward the animals.

Hardly had the company finished breakfast when the first outfit set off for the river. The girls stashed their things and boarded their schooner, waiting to take their place in line.

A movement on the edge of Amanda's vision brought a brief glimpse of Seth Holloway riding herd on the cattle. She did not allow her gaze to linger. Concentration was needed to maintain a proper distance between her mules and the wagon ahead.

"This is all so exciting," Sarah Jane gushed. "I never realized before how dead our camps were. All this organized bustle and activity. . ." Her words trailed off as she swiveled on the seat to look around the edge of the wagon.

"I liked the quiet," Amanda mused. Cutting a glance toward

71

Sarah, she found her too occupied in observing the surroundings to have heard. Amanda tightened her hold on the reins.

Soon enough, she glimpsed the belt of sycamores, oaks, and elms lining the banks of the awe-inspiring Big Blue, the sight and sound of which became more and more unnerving the nearer they got. She reined to a stop.

The long, slow process of crossing had already begun. A number of wagons dotted the opposite shore, and several more now inched across the swiftly flowing water at an upstream angle. Amanda noticed that some outfits drove right into the Blue, while others, at the river's edge, had men grunting and straining to remove the wheels so the beds could be elevated on wooden blocks. Still others were being hitched to double teams. Sarah jumped down without a word and walked ahead, where a handful of women stood watching the men at work.

Amanda's gaze returned to the brave souls traversing the roiling water, and her heartbeat increased. She tried to study the way the drivers retained control against the force of the current, knowing soon enough she would face that same challenge.

Sounds came from farther downstream, from bawling and balking cattle whose bobbing heads kept time with their sporadic movements. Several swung in wide-eyed frenzy to return to the riverbank, and a few of them lost their footing, only to be swept away by the rushing water. Amanda held her breath as outriders ignored those and quickly set to persuading the rest to continue on. She easily picked out Seth Holloway. With the determined set of his jaw and distinctive rigid posture, he stood out from the others. Watching him, she couldn't help but admire his mettle and strength.

"You'll be next, miss."

The low voice startled Amanda. She swallowed and obeyed the signal to pull up to the edge of the water. Sarah Jane climbed to the seat and clutched the edges, her knuckles white, as their schooner, somewhat lighter in weight than the more cumbersome Conestoga wagons, was checked over for the crossing.

Mr. Randolph stepped near, astutely reading the apprehension Amanda knew must be evident in her expression. "Don't worry, little gal. Just keep a firm hold on your animals. They're strong swimmers, an' I'll be right behind you, keepin' an eye out." With a grin of encouragement, he turned and strode to his own rig, parked off to one side so she could precede him.

Amanda tried to smile, but failed miserably as the men coaxed the skittish mules down the slippery bank and into the dark current that whooshed by unimpeded as it swirled over the animals' shoulders. They hee-hawed in protest, but began their unhappy swim.

The wagon bed rocked fore and aft, jouncing uncertainly on the choppy waves, and cold wetness splashed over the wooden sides to slosh about Amanda's feet. She couldn't have spoken if her life depended on it, but sent a frantic prayer aloft and held on for dear life.

The churning water surrounding them now seemed wide as an ocean. Hoping her own inexperience would not hinder the mules from following the rig ahead at a similar angle, Amanda clutched the reins, watching anxiously as the animals labored toward the opposite shore. Sarah, huddled beside her, kept her eyes closed the whole time. Amanda only hoped her sister was adding fervent prayers to her own.

An eternity later, forelegs and hind legs gained footing on the other bank, where men armed with strong ropes and other teams lent a hand and ushered the mules up to dry ground. It took all Amanda's stamina not to collapse in relief.

Moments later, the Randolph wagon followed and pulled alongside. A grin of satisfaction spread across the lined face of the older man, but his wife's was devoid of color. "Land sakes," she murmured. "Thank the good Lord we made that one!"

❧

As soon as Amanda had parked the wagon out of the way of the last remaining rigs and got down to unhitch the team, Sarah Jane climbed into the back and settled down with her journal:

> *Dear Diary,*
>   *I cannot even describe how good it feels to have come to the end of this busiest and most frightening day! Poor Mandy shook like a leaf when we had finally made it across the Big Blue—a curious name for a river flowing with such brown water! But when word reached us to make camp, both of us could have jumped for joy. Everyone else seemed grateful, too, since so many hours of daylight had been given to the effort of getting the entire assemblage to the westward side.*
>   *Now it is oddly peaceful. The animals graze contentedly on the shining grass, while the setting sun haloes the slim trees with a border of hazy gold. Most of the songbirds whose sweet trills lighten our journey have returned to their nests, and the twilight air is filled with the pungent smell of wood smoke. I wonder what tomorrow will bring.*

"That was some mighty fine driving you did earlier."

At the sound of Alvin Rivers' voice outside, Sarah quickly closed her book, set it down, and exited the wagon.

The young man's freckled face bore a grin from ear to ear at her sister, but his gaze immediately sought Sarah's. "If I hadn't had my own hands full helping out my aunt and uncle, I'd have gladly taken the reins for you."

Sarah saw Amanda smile her thanks.

"Mandy's almost as strong as Pa," she blurted.

Rolling her eyes, Amanda shook her head and began getting

into the wagon. "I'll see if there's enough dry wood and kindling to make a cook fire."

"Anyway," Alvin went on, "I'll see that the hubs get a good greasing after all that water."

"Why, how very sweet." Sarah tied her apron ties more snugly about her waist, then got out the cook pot while Alvin tended to the wheels. She returned to the fire Amanda was laying.

They both looked up at the sound of footsteps.

"No use botherin' with viddles tonight," Mrs. Randolph said. "One of our neighbors shot a fine pair of rabbits while the rest of us were comin' over the water. I'm just about to fry one of them right now, and you gals are more than welcome to join us. There's wild honey for the biscuits, too, thanks to him."

Coming after the trying day, the invitation was more than welcome. "We'd be delighted," Sarah said.

"If we can contribute something," Amanda quickly added. "Potatoes and carrots, at least? And may we watch?"

The older woman's bonnet dipped with her nod. "Don't mind if you do. Come anytime."

"Thanks ever so much. We'll be there soon as we put these things back inside." Amanda flashed a grin of relief at Sarah.

❧

At the close of the delicious meal, the girls made fast work of washing the dishes. When Alvin and some of his friends came by to claim Sarah for a walk, Amanda chose to linger over a second cup of coffee with their kind neighbor.

Twilight was deepening, and the cacophony of music made by the night creatures began to fill the air. . .pleasant sounds against the intermittent crying coming from the next wagon. Mrs. Randolph heaved a sigh. "Poor little thing starts up every night about this time."

Amanda dragged her gaze back to her hostess. "Where's her mama?" she couldn't help asking.

"That's a sorry tale." The older woman paused in raising her cup to her lips and slowly wagged her head. "While we were camped at Independence, the child's mother—scarcely more than a kid herself—was cavorting with her brood out in one of the fields, gathering wildflowers, racing to see who could pick the most. Running toward a real purty bunch of flowers, she turned to look over her shoulder at the little ones, and tripped over a root. Hit her head on a jagged rock, she did. Prit' near bled to death on the spot."

"How awful."

"Somebody went and fetched the doc right quick, but by the time he came, it was too late. Little gal was so weak she never even come to. She was in the family way, too, which didn't help matters." Mrs. Randolph gazed toward the motherless children.

A raft of sad memories flooded Amanda's mind, and her eyes swam with tears. She quickly blinked them away.

"Had ourselves our first funeral before we even left town," the older woman continued. "And now those precious babes are without a mother's love." Then, as if suddenly recalling that hadn't been the only death among the families gathering to migrate west this spring, she blanched. Her hand flew to her throat. "Mercy me. I'm as sorry as sorry can be, child. You losin' your own pa, too. I should be more careful to think before I talk."

Amanda reached to pat her gnarled hand. "It's all right. Truly. I've accepted Pa's passing on. We both have. And at least we're grown. What must those poor darlings be going through?" Her curiosity once again drew her stare toward the sobbing child—and met the somber gaze of the widowed father.

Amanda quickly averted her eyes, focusing on the half-empty cup in her hands. She gulped some of the lukewarm coffee. "What are the children's names, Mrs. Randolph? Perhaps there's something Sarah or I could do to help."

She nodded thoughtfully. "You know, there just might be, now that you mention it. The little girl's Bethany, as I recall. The boy, now. . .Hm." Frowning, she folded her arms over her generous bosom and tapped an index finger against her mouth. "Thomas, maybe. No, Timothy. Goes by the nickname Tad."

"And the father?" Amanda prompted, aware of a rising flush at her boldness.

The older woman seemed not to notice. "Name's Jared Hill. Seems a decent sort, leastwise from what we've gotten to know of him since we been on the trail. He's a mite standoffish."

Jared Hill. It suited him, Amanda decided—or did from a distance. She had yet to see him close up. The important thing was that the poor man had his hands full, and anyone with a sense of Christian duty should be more than willing to help in whatever small way she could.

By the time Amanda finished her coffee and made her way back to her own wagon, Bethany's sobs had ceased. She surmised that the children had been tucked in for the night. Mr. Hill, however, remained outside, kneeling in the circle of firelight, checking a section of harness. He looked up as Amanda neared.

She felt it only polite to smile. "Good evening."

"Evening, miss." Putting the traces aside, he rose, straightening his long limbs to tower a head above her. The eyes beneath his sandy hair appeared dark in the dim glow, their color indistinct, but a pronounced downward turn at the outer corners gave evidence of his grief.

Amanda stopped. "I—I couldn't help hearing your little girl cry."

He shrugged in resignation.

"So sorry to hear of your loss." Taking a step forward, she reached out her hand. "I'm Amanda Shelby, your new neighbor."

"Hill," he replied, shaking her hand. "Jared Hill. I'll do my best to see Bethy doesn't disturb you anymore."

"No!" Amanda gasped. "Please don't think—" Flustered that he'd mistaken her remark as criticism, she started over. "I—I only wanted to offer help. My sister Sarah's especially good with children. If there's anything we can do, please don't hesitate to ask."

His fingers raked through the tousled strands of his hair. "Well, thanks. Don't see as I need help, though. Or pity. We'll get by." One side of his mouth turned upward in the barest hint of a smile, softening his narrow face.

Amanda nodded. "Oh. But—Well, I just wanted to offer, that's all. Good night." At his nod of dismissal, she walked briskly away. . .trying not to feel utterly humiliated.

ten

"You'd be surprised what an interesting life Alvin has led," Sarah Jane declared as the wagon rumbled onward the following morning, the harness jangling in time with the clopping of the mules. "His great passion is art. Last year his aunt and uncle took him to Europe to art museums in Spain, Italy, France, and England, just to view the work of the great masters. He even showed me some of his own drawings. He's got wonderful talent."

"Oh, really?"

"Um-hmm. He's working on a book of sketches of the various terrain and landmarks along the trail. He's planning to try to interest a publisher in putting together a project of that sort for other folks thinking of heading west. Someday Alvin hopes to become a real artist. Maybe paint portraits, or—"

Her sister's sigh indicated she was only half listening.

Sarah paused and turned her head, a ringlet falling forward on her shoulder with the movement. She flicked it back. "You're awfully quiet this morning. Something wrong?"

Staring at her for a few seconds, Amanda finally spoke. "It's that man and the two young children, in the wagon behind the Randolphs."

"What about them?"

"The mother died accidentally back in Independence. The kids—especially the daughter—have taken it real hard."

At the sad news, Sarah's mouth gaped in dismay. "How very tragic. That would account for the crying I've heard from time to time. How old are those little ones?" She peered ahead, in the direction of their wagon.

"The boy, Tad, looks to be about four. Bethany must be three, or nearly so."

"Maybe we could help out somehow."

Amanda gave a soft huff. "That's what I thought, too. Only their father as much as told me to mind my own business."

Recalling her own first experience in the valley of the shadow of death, Sarah could easily identify with other people's sorrow. "Well, I'm sure he must not have meant to put you off so rudely. He might just be hurting, too. Remember how we felt when Mama died?"

Her elder sibling momentarily appeared lost in the sad memory of their own wrenching loss. "We knew our lives would never be the same. Nor had we expected to stand before another open grave so soon," she added with a pang of near bitterness.

"Maybe I'll make a doll for the little girl and take it by. She needs to be around women."

"I think that's a splendid idea." Amanda visibly relaxed.

Sarah lifted her gaze to the countryside, making mental notes she would enter into her diary later. There were considerably fewer trees since they'd crossed the river, no forests filled with glorious red-budded maples, no thickly wooded groves like those in the East, which seemed like nap on earth's carpet. Now she saw only the occasional solitary tree standing alone to face the elements.

The grasses, too, were taller, growing to a height of six or eight feet in the moist areas. The land itself was more open, allowing the wagons to spread out, some of them even traveling side by side as they meandered westward along the Little Blue River, a calm glistening ribbon of satin accented by the floral beauty of spring. Most of the womenfolk and youngsters had taken to walking now, in deference to the hard, springless wagon seats. Sarah often walked with them herself, taking part in the cheerful chatting as they gathered wood or colorful bouquets of wildflowers to pass the miles.

"Does Alvin Rivers have any other family?" Amanda asked, reverting to the previous topic.

"Not since he was quite young. His relatives have been raising him. He's pretty happy, though. Apparently they have a lot of money."

Her sister quirked a brow at her.

"Well, Alvin can't help that," Sarah said, her prickles up. "It isn't as if he lords it over anyone. He's just had advantages a lot of other young people have never enjoyed. Anyway," she added, lifting her chin, "we were quite comfortable ourselves not too long ago, if you recall."

"True."

"So maybe you shouldn't judge someone you don't even know."

Amanda flushed. "Yes, Mother," she said wryly.

"Well, if I'm going to make little Bethany a new doll, I'd best get to work." Sarah Jane swung her legs over the seat and retreated into the back, where she began rooting through the sewing supplies.

&

After a quiet supper of beans and fried mush, Amanda took the dirty dishes over to the river and knelt to wash them. The drowsy sultriness of the spring evening was crowned by the tranquil richness of a glorious sunset, which spread deepening violet shadows everywhere. She filled her lungs with the perfumes emitted by blue lupine and other flowers.

Splashing sounds from nearby ceased. Not twenty feet away, a man rose to his feet behind a curve in the riverbank that had concealed him from view. Stripped to the waist, he stood motionless for several seconds, his skin glistening like purest gold. When he pulled on his shirt, it clung to his muscular contours in a few enticingly damp places. Amanda caught herself staring.

So did he.

Her cheeks flamed.

Seth Holloway held her gaze, his expression altering not a whit as he fastened the last shirt button. He bent and retrieved his wide-brimmed hat, then nodded ever so slightly before plunking it on his wet head.

Amanda tried to quell the flush of heat in her face. Why hadn't she looked away, for pity's sake? She busied herself scrubbing the heavy iron frying pan in the flowing water with added vigor.

"Miss Shelby."

The sloshing water had covered the sound of his approaching footsteps. Amanda nearly lost her balance as she jerked her head to peer up at him. "Mr. Holloway. . ." She wondered what else to say, but needn't have been concerned. He was already striding away without a backward glance.

Thank heaven.

After returning to her rig, Amanda did her best to dismiss the mental picture of the wagon master from her mind. Had she been Sarah, she conjectured with a smile, she'd have flown right to her journal to pen flowery phrases of the magnificent vision Seth Holloway had made against the vibrant sky. But she wasn't Sarah. . .and anyway, a spinster shouldn't dwell on such nonsense.

With new resolve, she gathered her sewing and sat on a crate outside to enjoy the pleasant music and banter of camp as she hemmed the ties of another apron. It was quite gratifying to see the stock for the future store accumulating. Besides the half-dozen other aprons she had completed herself, Sarah had finished quite a pile of calico bonnets and flannel baby blankets. But with the younger girl's evenings so often taken up by Alvin Rivers and other young people, Amanda knew her own items would soon outnumber her sister's. Sarah had never lacked for friends. Amanda released a resigned breath.

A tall shadow fell across her work, blocking the glow from the big center fire. "Excuse me, miss?"

Startled, Amanda looked up to see that the low voice belonged to Jared Hill. "Yes?"

He removed the hat from his sandy hair and cleared his throat, then shifted his weight from one foot to the other, as if working up courage to speak. "I came to apologize. Had no call to be short with you when you asked after my kids. I know you meant well."

"Oh. Well, thank you. I took no offense, Mr. Hill." The statement wasn't quite true, but after Sarah's comments had put the whole thing into perspective, Amanda felt better about it and had been able to make allowances for the widower.

He nodded. "Well, I said my piece. I won't keep you from your chore." Offering a faint smile, he turned and walked away.

Amanda's spirit was lighter as she watched him go back to his own wagon. She had no intentions of forcing herself on the man's children, but it was nice to know that if she did have occasion to befriend them their father wouldn't shoo her away.

❧

Seth laid his hat on a rock, then spread out his bedroll and climbed in between the blankets, resting his head on his saddle. Face up, he clasped his hands behind his neck and stared idly at the myriad stars speckling the midnight sky. It reminded him of something. He searched his memory and grimaced. . .the Shelby girl had been wearing navy calico. That had to be it. He rolled over onto his side.

Truth was—and he'd be the last to admit it even to Red—it completely astounded him that those two young women had actually made it across the Big Blue on their own. Or rather, Amanda Shelby had done it on her own. Who would have expected a female of her tender age to have such pluck! A low chuckle rumbled from deep inside him.

On the other hand, he reasoned, that river was but one of numerous obstacles the train would face. There'd be plenty more opportunities for her to give up and turn back for Missouri. Yep, for all her faith that God would see her through, Seth knew they had to be merely brave words. Most people he'd met only put on that religious act to go along with their Sunday go-to-meeting duds. Come Monday morning, they all reverted back to their normal selves. She wouldn't be any different.

Course, when he'd been a tadpole, Seth had possessed quite the religious bent himself, much to his chagrin. His grandfather had seen to that. But after Gramps passed on, and Seth had grown up enough to see a few too many prime examples of church folk, he had wised up.

Too bad his brother Andrew hadn't been so perceptive, letting the wool be pulled over his eyes that way by that beautiful but scheming Eliza. Once a female had a man where she wanted him, she went in for the kill. Seth winced. That would be the day he would fall for any woman's goody ways or holy-sounding words. He was bright enough to see right through people, thanks to her.

Far in the distance, the lonely howl of a wolf carried on the wind. Seth raised his head to see the men on the night watch add wood and buffalo chips to the fires. He lay back down.

Enough time wasted thinking about women. There wasn't one of them worth the time of day.

But his mind refused to keep in line with his intentions. Seth found himself grinning. He had pretty near scared the prim Miss Shelby out of her skin, earlier. She'd all but toppled right into the Little Blue—and he could just imagine the sight she'd have made, all sputtering and flustered, water streaming off that long hair, her dress clinging to those fetching curves of hers. . .

Quickly reining in his wayward thoughts, Seth deliberately forced aside the vision of troubled green eyes that had a way of lingering in his mind as if he had no say in the matter. It was beginning to aggravate him how that at times he found himself comparing the variegated greens of the prairie grasses to the shade of those eyes. He'd best start keeping some distance between that gal and himself and concentrate on doing what he was hired to do—get these folks out west. Once he dumped them all off on that side of the world, he'd have no more cause to cross paths with that Shelby girl. End of problem. He squeezed his eyelids closed. . .but sleep was a long time coming.

eleven

Wood, water, and grass were plentiful along the friendly Little Blue, and so were flies and mosquitoes. Several evenings in a row, the wagons stopped to park alongside one another on its shady banks instead of drawing into the customary circle. A big common fire continued to draw forth fiddles, harmonicas, flutes, and lithe feet of emigrants eager to lose the weary monotony of travel in dancing and music. The menfolk, after tending to needed wagon repairs, would loll about and smoke their pipes, and the women would ignore the pesky insects long enough to visit and swap life stories.

During noon stops, Minnie Randolph had introduced Amanda to many of the other travelers. Added to the younger set she'd been meeting through Sarah and Alvin, Amanda now felt more a part of the company.

"I'll tell ye," Ma Phelps, a tall, rawboned woman, was saying as Amanda carried her sewing over by the great fire. "I've yet to find a better way to make johnnycakes."

A wave of murmured assents made the rounds, followed by a "Hello, Amanda-girl."

Amanda smiled and took a seat on the blanket that frail little Rosalie Bertram patted with her multiveined hand. The woman kept right on subject. "Hazel Withers just gave me a recipe for the most mouth-waterin' dried-apple pies t'other day. Y'all need to try it." Her nod loosened one of the skimpy braids in her graying coronet, and her nimble fingers quickly repositioned the hairpins.

Thin, weak-eyed Jennie Thornton squinted through her gold-rimmed spectacles at a nearby wagon as another muffled birthing scream contrasted sharply with the happy music. She exchanged knowing nods with the other women, then picked up the conversation again. "I'm still hankerin' for some of that buffalo steak the outriders rave about. Ain't even seen one o' them critters yet."

"We'll come across them soon enough, from what I hear," Mrs. Randolph said confidently. "Then there'll be meat to spare and enough to make jerky, to boot."

During a lull in the music, a soft slap sounded from the wagon confines, followed by a tiny cry. "Ohhh, that be our first young'un born on the trip," Ma Phelps breathed. "Shore hope the little angel makes it."

Several seconds of silent contemplation followed. Then the fiddles broke into another tune, and laughing couples linked elbows for the next jig.

Amanda felt a cool gust of wind. Pulling her shawl more closely about her shoulders, she noticed gathering clouds.

"Another shower's likely," Mrs. Randolph said. "Guess I'll go make sure everything's closed up nice and tight."

"Me, too." Amanda folded her project and went to shake out tarps and cover supplies in the wagon.

Sarah Jane came soon afterward. "Whew!" she breathed airily. "Sure is breezy out there. I hope it's just another nice rain like we had last night. I might be able to finish that doll for the little Hill girl. There's only the dress left to do." Reaching for the blue calico and the shears, she moved nearer to the lantern.

Amanda nodded. "It's turning out really cute. Where'd you get the hair?"

With a slightly embarrassed grin, Sarah flinched. "That old shawl of mine. . .the brown one. It was getting rather worn, so I pulled a thread and unraveled the bottom row."

"Bethany is sure to love her."

"You're not mad at me for being wasteful?"

"Heavens, no. It was very unselfish—and industrious of

you." Amanda picked up the small muslin figure and examined it more closely, from the tiny embroidered face to the ingenious woolen braids. It was sure to make one sad little girl perk up.

"I couldn't think of anything to give the boy," Sarah said.

"Well, I can!" Amanda jumped up. "Didn't Pa bring along that slingshot Johnny Parker gave him for luck?"

"Now that you mention it, yes, I think so. It's probably in with the wagon tools."

Amanda untied the canvas opening and went to dig through the tools in the jockey box. "It's here!" she exclaimed upon returning. "It brought us luck after all!"

Sarah Jane giggled. "Now, should I make the dress with full sleeves, or fitted? And it needs an apron, don't you think—which, by odd coincidence, just happens to be your specialty."

⁂

A few nights later, Mrs. Randolph again extended an invitation to supper. Sarah tucked the newly completed dolly deep into her pocket and handed the slingshot to Amanda to do the same, in case the opportunity arose to present the gifts. "What if they don't like them?" she asked, voicing her worst fear.

Amanda looked askance at her. "How could they not?"

"I don't know. I'm just wondering if we did right, is all. It really isn't interfering—is it?" Nervously she nibbled her lip, trying to recall when she'd last spent time with children.

"Don't be a goose. You're trying to befriend a lonely little girl, that's all."

"And her brother. And I'm not used to little boys. What if he doesn't like me?"

"Really, Sarah," Amanda sighed. "He doesn't have to like you, just the slingshot. He probably doesn't own one yet."

"You're right. I'm being silly. If they don't like me, I just won't bother them." *Ever again,* she added silently.

Coming up on the Randolph wagon, the tantalizing smells of crispy fresh fish and amazingly light biscuits greeted them.

Sarah swallowed the lump in her throat and drew a calming breath.

"Oh, you're here," Mrs. Randolph said warmly, accepting with a nod of thanks the cheese and the tin of peaches they'd brought along. "Sit right down. Everything's ready. Nelson? You say grace, will ya?"

He gave a gruff nod, settling his husky frame on one of the crates by their cook fire. "Almighty God, we thank you for the traveling mercies and for the food you provide us every day. Bless it now, we pray, and make us fit by it. Amen."

Raising her head, Mrs. Randolph whisked away an annoying fly. "I swear, such pests," she remarked, forking a portion of fish onto a plate and handing it to her husband. She passed the next serving to Amanda. "Hear tell somebody up front has come down with the fever."

The older man nodded gravely. "And once we come to the bad water spots, there'll be lots more of it."

A shudder went through Sarah. "What'll they do? The sick folks, I mean."

"Pull off by themselves, I 'spect," he answered. "Wait it out. See how they fare. Won't stop the rest of the train."

"It won't?" Amanda asked, obviously shocked. "That's hardly Christian."

"Mebbe. But it's what we all voted, back in Independence—and the only way to keep other folks from catchin' it. If they live, the next train along'll pick 'em up."

But what if they don't live? Sarah looked from one troubled face to the next. Things had gone so smoothly up until this point, she'd actually believed the whole trip would continue on in the same pleasant fashion. Now she felt a deep foreboding that this was just the beginning of woes to come. Who knew how many of this company would be called home to their eternal reward before ever reaching the western shores? Accepting the food Mrs. Randolph held out, she settled back in thought.

"We'll wash everything up, Mrs. Randolph," she heard Amanda say sometime later. Looking down at the plate in her own lap, Sarah noticed it was empty—yet she couldn't remember eating. Brushing crumbs from her skirt, she stood and helped her sister gather the soiled dishes, then walked woodenly beside her to the stream. "Mandy? Do you think we'll really make it out west? Truly?"

"All we can do is try," came her sister's honest answer. "We do our best, same as everybody else. . .and trust God, same as everybody else. In the end it's up to Him."

Sarah pondered the words in silence. "I—I haven't been keeping up with my prayers," she admitted at long last, regretting her laxness. "The days seem so busy. There's so little chance to find quiet times for prayer. I haven't touched Pa's Bible—haven't opened it once since Independence."

She felt an encouraging pat on her forearm. "Fortunately, the Lord's faithfulness isn't dependent on ours, Sissy, or we'd really be up a crick. It's never too late to get back to reading the Scriptures or talking to the Lord. He's always there."

"Good. I'm going to start praying and reading the Bible again tonight."

"And I'm going to be more faithful myself," Amanda replied. "Lots of nights I've been tired and skipped my prayers. That has got to stop. Right now."

New hope dawned in Sarah Jane as they finished the dishes and returned to the Randolphs'. No one could be sure about the future, that was true. But at least she would keep her hand in that of the One who, as the Bible said, knew the end from the beginning.

The train had stopped early for the night because of the onset of sickness. In the remaining daylight, Sarah peered expectantly at the next wagon. It was empty. But she caught Jared Hill on the edge of her vision, strolling along the river, a child's hand in each of his. "Mandy?" She nodded in the direction of the threesome. "Shall we go see them now?"

"Now or never, I suppose."

They took their leave and headed toward the water. Sarah Jane, slightly less at ease in the presence of a man easily ten years older than herself, had to muster all her courage when the tall widower glanced their way and stopped. "Good evening," she said politely. "I'm Sarah Jane Shelby."

"Miss Shelby," he answered with a nod, a look of surprise on his narrow face. "Jared Hill." Releasing Bethany's hand, he took the brim of his hat between his thumb and forefinger and dipped it slightly as he met Amanda's eye. "Miss."

"And who have we here?" Sarah added cheerily, more than glad to switch her attention to the little ones. She bent down to smile at the somber little girl.

Huge blue eyes grew even wider in the delicate face beneath fine blond hair. The child pressed closer to her father's leg.

"She's Bethy," her brother announced with four-year-old importance. "Her real name's Bethany. I'm Tad."

Sarah Jane beamed at the towhead, liking him at once— especially the sprinkling of freckles across his nose. "And you must be the big brother."

"Yep."

"Well, I'm very glad to meet you. I have a sister, too. Right here. This is my big sister. Amanda." She gestured behind herself as she spoke.

"Aw, I saw her lots of times. She comes to the Randolphs'."

"That's 'cause they're our friends," Sarah replied. "Do you have friends in the train?"

He shrugged. "Mama used to let me play with Sammy and Pete sometimes. They're over thataway." He pointed down the line. Then his bright expression faded. "We. . .we don't have a ma anymore."

Sarah noted the catch in his voice. "Oh, how sad," she murmured. "I know just how you feel. Our ma and pa live up in Heaven with Jesus, too. And you know what?" she added brightly. "I'll bet our mas are friends already."

"Think so?"

She nodded. "And they'd probably like us to be friends, too. What do you say?"

"I dunno." Tad sought his father's approval. "I guess."

"Good." Expelling a breath of relief, Sarah stood and motioned to Amanda. "We found something in our wagon you might like—that is—" She looked anxiously to Mr. Hill, feeling her color heightening. "—if your pa says you can have it."

Tentatively, Amanda held out the slingshot.

The lad's mouth dropped open. "Oh, boy! Can I keep it, Pa? Can I? Can I?"

No one could have resisted the pleading in that impish face, least of all his father. Nor could Sarah miss the depth of love that softened Jared Hill's demeanor as he gazed down at his young son. It warmed her heart. "Sure. I'll teach you how to use it, so you can do it right."

"Thank you! Thank you!" Tad said, awed by his new treasure.

Sarah touched his shoulder. "You're most welcome. Friends, remember?"

"Friends," he parroted.

Noting the way Bethany seemed drawn to the conversation, Sarah next knelt by her. "Would you be our friend, too, honey?"

The little girl pressed her heart-shaped lips together in mute silence, clutching her father's hand all the harder.

"It's all right," Sarah assured her. "Sometimes it takes a while to make a real friend. But my sister and I made something for you." Retrieving the dolly from her pocket, she offered it to Bethany.

The child stared longingly. Then, after glancing up and receiving her father's nod of approval, she slowly reached out and took it, hugging it for all it was worth.

Sarah Jane smiled. "She'll be a real true friend, you'll see. Pretty soon we'll come by and see you again, to make sure she's been minding her manners. Would you like that? My sister might even tell you a story. She knows lots of them."

A tiny smile curved her lips upward at the corners.

"Thank you, miss," Mr. Hill said with sincere gratitude. "Thank you both."

Completely charmed by the man's offspring, Sarah lifted her gaze to his and would have responded, but Amanda beat her to it.

"People like to help each other, Mr. Hill," her sister said kindly. "It's what neighbors are for. Do have a pleasant evening." With a smile at the children, she took Sarah's hand and started for their prairie schooner.

Sarah's backward glance revealed the tender sight of a father sweeping his two little ones up into his arms.

No crying issued from the Hill wagon that night.

twelve

Three more families fell prey to sickness the next day. Then two more. The number of wagons in the train began to dwindle as those afflicted dropped out of the column while the rest continued on—a concept the girls found utterly appalling. Even though other brave Good Samaritans willingly stayed behind to look after the sick—or worse, dig needed graves, the fate of the unfortunates weighed heavily on Amanda's mind. *O Lord,* she prayed fervently, *be with them. Please, take care of them. Bring them back to us.*

Weeks passed in tedious sameness as the wagon train rumbled through Nebraska in an upward slope of terrain so gradual the travelers were unaware they were going uphill until the bullwhackers' whips cracked more frequently and oxen and mules strained against the harness.

Amanda often watched her sister silently observing the world around them and knew she was memorizing scenes, sounds, and sensations to record the minute they stopped for the noon meal or evening camp. From the various passages the younger girl had already related to her, Amanda knew entries in Sarah's journal chronicled how the grass along the route now grew shorter, the trail sandier, and the weather more changeable, and the way a day could dawn in mild and colorful splendor—only to cloud over and turn cold, pelting the travelers with rain or even hail. But with spring's fragile beauty lingering into early summer, the younger girl's spirits—along with everyone else's—remained high. Especially considering the plentiful elk and antelope to provide respite from the daily fare of smoked or salted meats.

On one of the meal stops along the arid plain between the Platte River and the low hillsides lining the valley, Amanda watched Sarah scribbling furiously in her diary. "Does it help much?" she teased.

Sarah stopped writing and crimped her lips together. Then she smiled. "Well, not that I'm likely to ever forget the way the wagon wheels screech in protest with every turn lately—or the huge clouds of dust they throw up into our faces. But I thought I'd jot it down for posterity anyway. At least we can breathe through our handkerchiefs or apron hems. I'll be glad to see the end of this section."

Amanda had to giggle.

One afternoon, lulled into a state of half-awareness by the clopping of the animals, Amanda was brought rudely back to the present by an ear-shattering crack. Horrified, she watched as the wagon ahead tipped crazily, then crashed to the ground over its splintered rear wheel. She struggled to maintain control of her own startled mules, then steered cautiously around the disabled outfit so she wouldn't be in the way of the men who would immediately assist in replacing the wheel.

"That's the second one today," Sarah Jane whispered.

Amanda nodded. "The dryness of the air is making the wood shrink. I wonder when our turn will come."

"Alvin says that when he finishes helping his uncle tonight, he and his friend Jason will soak our wheels in the river."

Despite the comforting news, Amanda's unrest persisted. So many, many miles lay ahead. Could she have been wrong to presume the Lord wanted her and Sarah to go west after all? Pa had often teased her about her stubborn streak. What if she had placed her own will above God's? The two of them might make the entire trip—only to meet with unhappiness and misfortune in the Oregon Territory! She couldn't help recalling the incident in the Bible where the Israelites demanded meat in the wilderness rather than the manna God so graciously provided. He granted their request, but sent leanness to their souls.

"Let's teach the kids some songs tonight."

"Hm?" Amanda swallowed, forcing aside her disquiet.

"I said," Sarah Jane repeated, "Bethany and Tad might like to learn some songs."

With her mind occupied by more serious concerns, Amanda merely shrugged. "Sure."

"Good. Tonight when we go to see them, I'll take my guitar." Reaching around for the instrument, Sarah unwrapped the sheet shrouding it, plucked a few strings, then adjusted the tuning pegs. "What with all my sewing and visiting, it's been ages since I practiced. I wonder which tunes they might particularly like." Her face scrunched in thought as she strummed a chord.

The slightly flat tones brought a smile to Amanda. So did the realization of how the children had grown to welcome their visits. It seemed a fair exchange when Mr. Hill offered to look after repairs on both wagons while she or Sarah— sometimes both—took the little ones for walks along the rocky outcroppings on the hills or near the shallow river.

But when this evening finally came, Amanda's pensive mood knew the further aggravation of a dull headache, precluding even the enjoyment of the usual camp music. She left the visiting and singing to her sister and strolled somewhat apart from the train.

The night breeze rustled the dry grasses beneath the huge dome of starry sky as she walked, and nightly cricket sounds blended with the familiar lowing of the cattle. Amanda sank to her knees and clasped her hands. *Dear Father,* began her silent plea. To her frustration, no further words would come. She loosened her shawl and lay back, losing herself in the display of the twinkling host so high above her. . .almost wishing she had never left Independence.

❧

"Isn't that the Shelby gal?" Red asked, with a jut of his chin toward the open prairie beyond the camp perimeter.

Seth followed his friend's gesture as if it was news to him

. . .as if he hadn't seen Amanda's slender form depart, hadn't observed nearly her every step. "Probably. Just like her to go off by herself as if there isn't a wolf or rattler for miles."

"Want me to go bring her back?"

"Naw." Rubbing a hand across the bridge of his nose, Seth let out a slow breath. "I'll just keep an eye on her from here."

"Don't appear as if you're the only one. I've noticed a certain widower's a lot less sorrowful lately, since her an' her sister have been ridin' herd on those little ones of his. I s'pose it would solve more'n a few problems if he hitched up with one of 'em."

Seth huffed. "No never mind to me." But the confirmation of a niggling suspicion sank slowly to the pit of his stomach.

❧

"This a private party?"

Amanda bolted upright with a start. "Not at all, Mr. Hill. I was just looking for some quiet."

He sank down a few feet away, propping an elbow on one bent knee and followed her gaze to the starry heavens. "Does get pretty noisy some nights."

Neither spoke for several seconds.

"Don't you think it's time you quit being so formal?" he finally asked. "We're not strangers anymore."

Amanda regarded him in the twinkling light. "No, we aren't strangers."

"Friends, then?"

"I guess so."

"Then it's Jared. And Amanda—unless you say otherwise."

She shook her head, then looked away. Everyone needed friends. There was no reason to keep always to herself. But she wasn't silly enough to expect—or even desire—anything more than friendship again. Once was enough. And anyway, she assured herself resolutely, Jared Hill couldn't possibly be putting more into this relationship than there was. It was far too soon for him to even be thinking about replacing his dear late wife. Amanda relaxed and began idly plucking at the stiff grass. Another span of silent seconds passed.

Jared raked his fingers through his hair. "Helped two young fellows take your wheels down to soak in the river a while ago. Should keep you going a ways now."

She smiled. "I don't know how we'd make it but for the kindness of folks on the train. Thanks."

"Least I can do after what you and Sarah have done for my boy and girl." He filled his lungs, quietly releasing the breath through his nostrils.

"They really miss their mama."

Jared didn't respond immediately, but Amanda felt his gaze switch to her. "Well, guess I'll head back." Standing up, he offered a hand.

She grinned and placed hers inside his more calloused one, and he raised her effortlessly to her feet. They walked in companionable silence back to camp.

❧

The crossing of the shallow but fierce, mile-wide south fork of the Platte went without mishap. Advised about the threat of quicksand, no one ignored the order to water all animals beforehand to prevent them from stopping in the middle of the chocolate-colored river.

But Amanda would never forget the terror that seized her some miles later, poised on the brink of Windlass Hill. She and Sarah Jane gaped down the steep grade, watching the harried descent of other wagons. Even with the back wheels chained to prevent them from turning, and with dozens of men tugging on ropes to slow the downward progress, gravity sucked mercilessly at the rigs skidding and sliding to the bottom. To the girls' horror, midway down the slope, one outfit broke free of restraint. Amid screams of onlookers, it teetered and toppled over the side, careening end over end till it came to rest, a shattered heap of rubble. For a moment of stunned silence, no one so much as breathed.

"That does it," Jared Hill announced, climbing up to the seat and taking the reins from Amanda. "No way I'm gonna let the two of you try this one." A jerk of his head ordered the girls out to walk with the other women. "See that my kids keep out of the way, will you?" He wrapped the traces firmly around his hands and eased the mules forward, already applying pressure to the brake. Neither girl could bear to watch their schooner's descent to the reaches below.

When the nerve-wracking day came to a merciful end with the arrival of the last wagon in Ash Hollow, the cool, bountiful meadow at the base of Windlass Hill seemed a glorious oasis. The very air was fragrant with the mingled perfume of the wild rose and scents of other flowers and shrubs in the underwood of majestic ash and dwarf cedar trees.

"Why, there's actual shade!" Sarah Jane cried, as she and her small group reached the bottom of the hill. Taking Bethany and Tad by the hand, she bolted ahead of Amanda and Mrs. Randolph, with the children in her wake. Under the green canopy of a huge ash, she swooped the little girl up and swung her around. Tad ran circles around them both.

Mrs. Randolph joined in with their gleeful laughter. "I declare! It's the Garden of Eden, that's what it is." Joining Sarah, she kicked off her worn boots and wiggled her plump toes in the silky grass, her expression almost dreamlike.

Amanda's gaze drifted to the center of the meadow, where prattling little streams merged together in a translucent pond, sparkling now in the late afternoon sun. She hadn't realized how thirsty she had been. The last truly decent water had been long since passed. Glancing around, she spotted her wagon parked beside Jared Hill's and hurried over to get a pitcher.

Her neighbor was tightening the straps on his rig's canvas top when she approached. "Some place, huh?" he said pleasantly. "Almost feels like we deserve it after a day like today."

Amanda laughed lightly and clambered aboard her schooner. Jared's low voice carried easily through the bowed fabric.

"Wagon master says we're stopping here for a day or two. Plenty of folks have a whole bunch of new repairs to see to. And most everyone will pitch in to help the Morrises salvage what they can from their wreck."

"That was truly a horror," Amanda said, emerging with the coveted pitcher in hand. "On the way down the hill, at least half a dozen ladies speculated on which of them could best make room for the family, bless their hearts. And I couldn't be more grateful for a day of rest. Tomorrow's Sunday anyway, isn't it?"

"Come to think of it, you're right."

"Pa! Pa!" two young voices called out above their scampering footsteps. They made a beeline for him and flung their arms around his long legs.

Gratified at the sweet display of affection, Amanda averted her gaze and hopped to the ground.

Sarah Jane stepped beside her at the spring. "Alvin's aunt has invited me to supper. Do you mind, Mandy?"

"Of course not. Just don't stay out late."

"Yes, Mother." With a wry grimace, her sister joined her curly-haired escort.

Oh well, Amanda decided, watching the pair walk away, I've been wishing for solitude lately. This should provide a nice quiet night of sewing.

Or praying, her mind added. What she needed above all was to know inner peace again. There had to be some way to find it.

thirteen

The summer sun warmed the faithful flock gathered in the meadow for Sunday service on a curious collection of wooden chairs, crates, blankets, and the odd fallen log. The breeze rustling the leaves in the glen was gloriously free of the mosquitoes that had plagued the encampment late last evening. Now the voices blended in harmony with the fiddle and harmonica.

Amanda had known "Abide With Me" most of her life but had never paid close attention to the words. But as Sarah had pointed out a week ago, it must have been a lot of folks' favorite, the way it got requested almost every Sunday. Going into the second verse, Amanda listened even as she sang:

> "Swift to its close ebbs out life's little day;
> Earth's joys grow dim, its glories pass away;
> Change and decay in all around I see;
> O Thou who changest not, abide with me."

Certainly this trip had brought about drastic changes. Amanda surmised that other folks' dreams of a new life had probably been every bit as grand as hers. Yet despite the fact that many of them had already lost friends and loved ones to sickness or accident, they found strength to continue on. Lonely, saddened, they somehow remained hopeful. It had to be of tremendous comfort to know that the Lord stayed ever constant. She observed the peaceful countenances of some of the folks within her range of sight and went on to the third stanza:

"I fear no foe, with Thee at hand to bless;
Ills have no weight, and tears no bitterness.
Where is death's sting? Where, grave, thy victory?
I triumph still, if Thou abide with me."

When Amanda saw a woman blot tears on her apron as she sang, her own eyes stung, rendering her unable to voice the lyrics herself. She finally managed to regain her composure for the final lines:

"Heaven's morning breaks, and earth's vain shadows
    flee;
In life, in death, O Lord, abide with me."

Never again would that hymn carry so little meaning. Amanda realized for the first time that it had not been her own strength that had held her together after the loss of her parents. It had been the Lord all along. His strength, His faithfulness—and those, without a doubt, loving answers to her mama and papa's faithful prayers. Humbly she bowed her head and breathed a prayer of gratitude.

She opened her eyes to see the jug-eared man most folks had started calling "Deacon Franklin" rise from his seat and move to the vacant spot the fiddler left behind at the close of the song.

"Folks," he began. "As you've figured out by now, I'm not much of a preacher. But like I said before, I love the Lord, and I love His Word. Thought I'd read a favorite verse that has been a real blessing to me for a lot of years. It's in Romans, the eighth chapter, verse twenty-eight." He opened his worn Bible to the page his finger had held at the ready. " 'And we know that all things work together for good to them that love God, to them who are the called according to his purpose.' "

Looking up from his text, he scanned the rapt faces before him and smiled gently. "There's hardly a one of us who hasn't at some time or other questioned the Lord's doings. Especially these last hard weeks, as we've all of us watched helplessly at the hardships that came to folks who were once part of this travelin' family of ours."

Bonneted heads nodded, and murmurs circulated in the ranks.

"But in spite of all that comes by," the leader continued, "whether sickness, or death, or accident, I know we can still trust God. There's no lack of people in this world who don't give Him any part of their lives a'tall. Can't help wonderin' what gets them through the hard times, or where they turn for help. There'd be none to find if we just threw up our hands and turned our backs on the One who made us, the One who is workin' out His purposes through all the circumstances of our lives. Yes, I said *all*," he injected without a pause. "There's not one among us who's here by chance."

Amanda's ears perked up.

"It doesn't make a lick of difference what made us choose to make this trip," the speaker said with a firm nod. "What does count is that the God who brought us here will never let us down. Think about that today and tomorrow—and all the tomorrows yet to come. Trust your well-being to the Lord and keep a good hold on His strong hand. And whatever effort you've been givin' to complainin' about hills or rivers or dust or mud, spend instead in thankin' God for takin' you through it. If you see somebody beside you startin' to sag, bolster him up with a kind word—or better yet, lend a hand. This journey is gonna take all of us pullin' together, helpin' one another along."

Deacon Franklin rocked back onto his heels and tucked his Bible under one arm, and a twinkle in his eye accompanied his smile. "Well, that's all I have to say this morning. Be sure and enjoy this nice purty restin' spot the Good Lord put here just for us, right enough! Now, let's close in prayer."

A new calmness began to flow through Amanda's being as she closed her eyes. The words hadn't come from behind a proper pulpit. The speaker was not in reality a man called to be a preacher to the masses, and the speech hadn't even been what one might term a sermon. Yet her spirit felt strangely comforted and encouraged. She almost felt like dancing.

❧

Behind the furrowed gray trunk of a swamp ash, Seth flicked a crumbled leaf through his fingers and headed for the cook wagon. No sense having Red catch him listening in on a sermon, that's for sure! It wasn't worth the endless mocking that was certain to follow.

It beat all, though, how this bunch seemed to handle the misfortunes and tragedies that struck so relentlessly now. Unlike some of the travelers he'd taken west in previous years, these folks even seemed sincere in believing what that farmer told them. Took it right to heart. Of course, Grandpa had been that way, too, he remembered. Never once doubting the Good Book or the Lord above. Seth could still picture the shock of white hair above the aged face, could still see the piercing eyes that seemed to see clear into a person's soul. The old man's voice contained a gravelly quality, as if preaching had used it up somewhere along the way. But those long arms of his, which could spread so wide to make a point, had felt mighty warm and strong wrapped around a young boy's shoulders.

An unbidden memory came to the fore of times he and Drew had ridden double on old Lulabelle while Gramps took them along on a preaching trip. He'd sit the two of them right in the front row, where one look could still their squirming through the longest sermon. Seth smiled, knowing if he thought back far enough, he'd have to admit there was a time he thought of becoming a circuit-riding preacher himself! Wouldn't Red get a kick out of that!

Seth emitted a ragged breath. A lot of years had passed since then. He'd ended up on a far different path. . .but a very small part of him was starting to hunger for the kind of sincere faith he'd known as a young lad.

ஐ

"Sarah?" Alvin extended a hand as they left the service. "Will you come for a walk with the rest of us? Aunt Harriet wants me to pick her some currants and chokecherries."

She smiled, but shook her head, mildly disappointed. "Can't. I promised Bethany I'd help her make a flower crown."

"You could do that later."

Sarah felt compelled to refuse. "I wouldn't want to disappoint her, Alvin. She's only a little girl, and I—"

"—sure spend a lot of time with kids that aren't even related to you," he finished. "You used to be more fun."

Ignoring the critical note in her friend's usually jovial tone, Sarah just nodded. "I still like to have fun, Alvin. But sometimes there are other things that need doing. Anyway, it's hard to resist a pair of big blue eyes."

"Exactly." A rakish gleam lit the hazel depths of Alvin's. "Won't I ever get to finish that sketch I started of you?"

"Sure you will. We'll have plenty of time together, you'll see. Now, I really must go. Thanks for the invitation, though."

"Right." The edge of his lip took on a strange curl before he turned and strode away.

Almost wishing she'd accepted, Sarah stared after him. She felt Amanda step to her side.

"It's really sweet of you to turn down an afternoon's frolic just to keep a little girl happy."

"I promised," Sarah Jane said simply.

"I know. I'm very proud of you."

"Really?"

A blush tinted her sister's cheeks. "Well, it's just— You know. When we first spoke of coming west, I was afraid you'd get in one pickle after another. But you're changing by the day."

Sarah cocked her head back and forth. "I imagine it's called growing up."

"I suppose. Just wanted you to know, I like the change."

"Thanks, Sissy. And while we're at it, I'd like to say I'm sorry for not being more help sewing, cooking, driving. . .I've let you down. That's going to change, too."

❧

When the company again took up the journey, a new, lighter mood prevailed. . .until the nine-year-old Thornton boy, riding the tongue of his family's wagon on a dare, plunged under the wheels shortly after departing Ash Hollow. An unexpected funeral took place that noon. The little body was laid to rest in a grave dug right beneath the rutted trail. The wagons to follow would pack the earth hard again, too hard for wolves to ravage.

And another new baby came into the world that night.

" 'The Lord giveth, and the Lord taketh away,' " Mrs. Randolph muttered as Amanda poured a cup of coffee for them both outside the schooner. "My old heart goes out to Jennie. He was their only boy, you know. The others are girls. He'd have been a big help when they got settled in Oregon."

Sipping her own coffee, Amanda could barely swallow.

"Say, these are right fine apple fritters your Sarah made."

"She's been—well, we've been practicing."

"And it shows."

"Thanks to you."

The older woman sloughed off the compliment. "Pshaw. You'd have picked up all the cookin' you needed in time anyway."

"Even if that's true," Amanda said, patting her friend's arm, "you surely made it much easier for us. We both appreciate it." She paused with a smile. "I don't know if I'm going to want to part with you when we get to the California Trail and you and Mr. Randolph head off to go be with your sons. What did you say their names were?"

"Nelson Junior an' Charlie," the older woman said proudly. "Don't mind admittin', though, if I had my druthers I'd still be back home in our Allegheny Mountains. At my age, thought of sittin' in my rockin' chair in front of a cracklin' fire was soundin' mighty pleasurable. But when Nelson, the oldest, got the notion to go see what lay beyond the hills, he up and took our other'n and they lit out. Ended up in northern California—far as they could get—then convinced their pa an' me to come, too. One of 'em might even come to meet us partway."

Amanda smiled. "Well, it'll truly be a whole new life for you then—without having to start from scratch, like most of us. You might even arrive to discover they've built you a nice little cabin, fireplace and all, complete with a rocker."

"If not, I brung my own along," she admitted with chagrin. "Didn't want to take a chance. It was my own ma's. Our two boys got rocked on it, so did our girl. Course, little Rosie wasn't with us too long. . ." Blinking away a sudden sheen in her faded blue eyes, she looked Amanda up and down, then tapped a crooked finger against her bottom lip in thought. "You'd make our Charlie a pretty fair wife, if you don't mind my sayin' so."

Amanda, having raised her mug for another sip, swallowed too quickly and choked instead.

"There, there," her neighbor crooned, thumping her on the back. "Just take a deep breath, now. You'll be right as rain." Barely stopping, she resumed the conversation where she'd left off. "Nelson Junior took himself a wife out west. Found her in Sacramento. Name's Cora. But our Charlie's still loose."

Amanda had to giggle.

Barely stopping for breath, Mrs. Randolph rambled on. "Course, I know you an' Sarah Jane have high hopes of openin' a store an' all—which sounds fine. Real fine. I think folks will need new clothes, just like you said." Handing Amanda her empty mug, she ambled to her feet. "Well, I'd best be gettin' back. But store or no store, give some thought to my Charlie, would you? Don't mind tellin' you, a body could do worse havin' you for a daughter-in-law."

At this, Amanda couldn't resist hugging her. "Or you for a mother-in-law. Thanks for coming by."

fourteen

For three more weeks, the train continued along the sandy banks of the North Platte. A mile or two off to the left and right, two lines of sand hills, often broken into wild forms, flanked the valley beneath the enormous sky. But before and behind, the plain was level and monotonous as far as the eye could see.

"Nights are growing colder now," Sarah read to Amanda from her open journal. Tired of walking, she had hopped aboard for a short rest. "Even though it's still the dead of summer, the temperature continues to drop as we go higher. Soon we'll glimpse the peaks of the Laramie Mountains, I'm told, their frosted caps sparkling diamond-white against crystal blue sky." Amanda smiled to herself. Her sibling had always possessed a gift for writing, and the abundant wonders of the trail brought that talent to the fore. More and more often she would look up after finishing a paragraph, obviously eager to share her latest entry—whether it chronicled the pesky sand flies that replaced the mosquitoes everyone found such a torment during the nights at Ash Hollow, the thunderous sound of a buffalo herd on the move, the delicate appeal of grazing antelope, or how the landscape was becoming more brown than green and was empty now of timber, sage, and even dry grass.

And Amanda couldn't help noting a vast improvement in the younger girl's vocabulary as the miles passed. Sarah's association with artist Alvin Rivers revealed itself in new, eloquent words and phrases she now used in her diary. She did not share all of her innermost thoughts concerning Alvin, but had no qualms about revealing passages about special times she spent with the Hill children.

But best of all, in Amanda's estimation, had been her sister's written accounts of the various landmarks whose unique formations had come into view while still a whole day's travel away. Sarah painted word pictures. . .visions of glorious rainbow hues cast over the towering shapes by the ever-changing play of sunlight between dawn and dusk. She likened the mounds of stone to castles and ships and slumbering animals. Amanda felt those images would remain forever in her mind.

She truly appreciated the diversions in the tiresome journey. More than once she had caught herself straining for a glimpse of the wagon master and that gray horse of his, then would quickly chide herself for such foolishness. Having Sarah's daily narratives to concentrate on kept her wandering thoughts in line.

Not long after the snow-patched Laramie Mountains appeared on the far horizon, cheers and whistles came from the front of the company. Sarah, walking beside the wagon, jumped onto the slow-moving vehicle, then craned her neck to see around the outfits ahead. "Mandy! It's Fort Laramie! And I'm just covered with trail dust. I do wish we had time to freshen up." She grabbed the hairbrush from a basket beneath the seat and tugged it through her curls, then removed her apron and fluffed out her skirt. "Do I look all right? I hear we'll be able to replace the flour and other supplies."

"If there's any to be had after everyone else restocks, of course," Amanda reminded her. "No doubt it'll cost us dearly."

"Well, whatever the price, we'll have to bear it. We've still a long, long way to go." She paused. "Oh! Look at the sparkly river—and all the Indian shelters everywhere!"

Amanda nodded, her gaze lost in the sharp contrast between the Black Hills, thick with cedar, and the area's red sandstone. Speckled with sage, the sparse grass was turning yellow. She flicked the reins to keep pace with the others, urging the mules up the steep bank leading to the entrance of the fort, where huge double doors had been raised to permit the train to enter.

"Not as impressive as I expected," Sarah murmured, nearing the cracked, decrepit adobe walls. But exhaling a deep breath, she waved to the sentry perched in the blockhouse erected above the gateway as they pulled inside, where Indians in buffalo robes stared down at the new arrivals from perches on the rampart. After stopping the team, Amanda glanced around the interior. Long, low buildings stretched out in a large circle, forming the walls around a great open area crowded with Indians and traders. Among the horde strolled lean, rough-looking frontiersmen, their long rifles at the ready for any sign of trouble. The noise and bustle of the bargaining reminded Amanda of Independence. Within moments, Alvin Rivers came to offer a hand to Sarah, then to Amanda. "Word has it we're to rest here for two whole days. Mind if your sister and I explore a bit?"

Amanda smiled as she stepped to the ground and arranged her skirt. "Not at all. I'll likely do some of that myself, once I've tended the animals." That evening, the replenished emigrants joined forces and shared their bounty with some of the fort folk. The men quickly assembled makeshift banquet tables from wagon boards propped up on barrels, and the women filled them end to end with heaping platters of roast hen, antelope, buffalo steak, fried fish, and all manner of vegetables and breads, followed by a delectable assortment of berry pies, tarts, and jelly cakes.

Much laughter and banter passed to and fro as everyone caught up with the latest news from back east. Word regarding conditions of the trail ahead brought raised brows and shakes of the head, then expressions of resignation and determination.

When at last every appetite was sated, an even grander celebration began. Double the usual number of instruments broke forth in song, aided by clapping hands and stomping feet, which drew the more energetic souls to frolic.

"You should go have some fun with the other young folks, Amanda," Mrs. Randolph said, gesturing after them. "Leave the cleanin' up to us old fogies."

"I'd rather not. Really," Amanda assured her friend. "I prefer to be useful." But a small part of her wished she still felt as young as Sarah and her friends. In an effort to tamp down the wistful longing, she began humming along with the happy tune while she worked.

"Land sakes," Mrs. Randolph exclaimed, putting leftover bread and biscuits into a sack. "I'm full near to burstin'!"

"Me, too," Ma Phelps chimed in. "I might never take another bite of food as long as I live. Or at least till tomorrow." She guffawed at her own levity.

Amanda had to grin as she gathered some half-empty tins and scooped the remaining portions of the pies into them. She licked berry juice from her sticky index finger and glanced around for another chore.

Disassembling tables with some of the other men a few yards away, Jared Hill looked up and caught her gaze with a smile. "Care to go for another stroll with me and the kids?" he asked.

Spending time with the little family had become a commonplace activity by now. She shrugged a shoulder and nodded.

A sudden movement in the shadows between two of the warehouses revealed Seth Holloway as he spun on the heel of his boot and stalked away.

❧

"Oh, Alvin," Sarah breathed, flipping through his sketchbook as they sat on crates outside his uncle's wagon, somewhat apart from the noise. "These are truly wonderful." She studied a sketch of a vast buffalo herd, then one of a valley filled with the animals' whitened bones and skulls, before turning to the more pleasing views of Chimney Rock and the majestic Courthouse Rock. "I was certain nothing could be more beautiful than your drawing of Devil's Gate, but this. . ." She leaned closer to examine his most recent landscape— Fort Laramie and the Laramie River, with the Black Hills as a backdrop. She ran her fingers lightly over one of the bastions.

"What about these?" he asked tentatively, taking down a second drawing pad and holding it out.

Sarah observed the peculiar gleam in the young man's blue eyes as she took the proffered book from him and opened it. The warmth of a blush rose in her face. Page after page presented renditions of her. All were very good. . .and almost too flattering. She swallowed. "But I never posed for these."

"You didn't have to. Everywhere I look, I see you. Don't you know that by now?" Taking the sketches from her unresisting fingers, he stood and drew her to her feet, encircling her with his long arms.

He had been a perfect gentlemen over the hundreds of miles the train had traveled, almost always sharing her company with other young people. Now, Sarah's heart raced erratically as she felt Alvin's breath feather her neck. "Please, don't—" she whispered.

But his head moved closer, until his lips brushed hers. "You're so beautiful, sweet Sarah. I could spend my whole life drawing you, painting you. You could become famous right along with me."

Though the last was said in a jesting tone, his previous remarks had been anything but so. Uncomfortable, she drew away. Mixed emotions—confusing emotions—rushed through her being. "But we're friends. . .Neither of us knows for sure where our paths will lead at the end of this trip."

Alvin's expression did not alter a whit. "It's afterward I'm thinking about, Sarah. You, me, the two of us. Forever. I won't be a pauper when we reach Oregon, you know, unlike most folks. I'll have a lot to offer. . .and I want you to think about that." He took one of her hands in his and pressed it to his lips.

Sarah searched his eyes, afraid to utter the question closest to her innermost longings. How could she ask something so deeply intimate as whether or not he ever wanted children? She didn't know him well enough yet—and she wasn't sure she truly wanted more than friendship from him. . .now or ever.

Gently she pulled her fingers from his grasp. "I—I—" But words failed her. She turned and ran blindly for the wagon.

❧

"Sure is a pleasant evening," Jared said.

Amanda, walking by his side, could only agree as she drank in the star-dusted night sky, the warm lantern glow from the many rooms and buildings of the fort. She smiled after Bethany and Tad, who were skipping ahead of them. "Everyone's so happy to have their barrels refilled. And to rest, I might add."

He nodded, and his gaze returned to his children. "They're a lot happier, too. Thanks to you. . .and your sister."

Something in Jared's tone sounded an alarm in Amanda. She moistened her lips. "Well, the whole train was eager to lend a hand—" she began.

"But no one did, except you."

Amanda felt an inward shiver and drew her shawl tighter around her shoulders.

"They're almost their old selves, now," he went on. "The way they used to be."

Determined to keep the conversation casual, Amanda responded only generally. "It's nice to see them smiling."

"I sure don't have to tell you they think a lot of you, Amanda. And so d—"

"I think we should head back now, Jared, don't you?" she blurted. "Bethy! Tad! Time to go." Grabbing them one by one in a hug as they ran to her, Amanda turned them around and pointed them toward the clustered wagons. "March."

"Like soldiers?" Tad asked. "Yes, sir!" Immediately he

straightened to his full height and puffed out his chest. "Hup, two, three, four. . .hup, two, three, four."

A giggling Bethany did her best to mimic her older brother's longer strides. The effect was enchantingly comical.

Grateful for the lightened mood, Amanda picked up the pace to discourage further conversation. This night she would be spending more time than usual at her prayers.

ঌ

"Ah! Some real, actual rest. At long last." Red yawned and straightened his legs as he leaned against the wheel of the supply wagon and crossed his arms. "Let somebody else do the lookin' out, for a change." He tugged his hat over his eyes.

In no mood to make small talk, Seth only grimaced. The rowdy music was giving him a headache. Above the camp smells he could detect rain coming. And he detested wasting travel time when early snow could close the mountain passes.

His pal plucked the hat away and leaned his head to peer at him. "Boy, you sure do have a burr under your saddle."

"Why do you say that?"

"Oh, nothin'. 'Cept, you ain't said a word for the last three hundred miles or so, that's all."

"Nothing to say."

Red nodded, a lopsided smirk pulling his mustache off kilter.

"Look. Do me a favor, will you?" Seth rasped. "If you want to talk about trail hazards or the trip in general or the storm that's coming, go ahead. We'll plan accordingly. Otherwise, clamp those jaws of yours shut and give me some peace."

"Right, boss. Will do." With a mock salute, Red replaced his hat over his eyes and nose and resumed his relaxed pose.

A pair of pregnant minutes ticked by.

The hat fell to Red's lap. "Er, get the letter that was waitin' for you?"

Seth slanted him a glare.

"I just asked. None of my business, I know. Even if it was

wrote by a woman. Same last name as yours, I noticed."

Releasing a lungful of air all at once, Seth lurched to his feet, whacking dust off the seat of his britches.

Red jumped up, too, and grabbed Seth's sleeve. "Hey, buddy, I ain't pryin'."

"Oh, really?"

"Sure. Your brother's got the same last name, too. Figure it must be from her. That wife of his."

"So?"

"So nothin'. Figure you know what you're doin'." He rubbed his mouth. "Just hope you're not foolin' around with—"

Seth's fist sent his partner sprawling backward in the dust. Immediately he regretted the hasty act and leaned over to help Red up. "Sorry. I didn't mean that. And I'm not."

Kneading his jaw and working it back and forth, Red shrugged and gave a nod. "Didn't really think you were." He smirked again. "You really hated that woman Andrew married, didn't you?"

"Hated her?" Seth looked him straight in the eye. "On the contrary, pal. I was in love with her, but she refused me." Turning, he left Red gaping after him as he walked away.

fifteen

Ten exhausting days after leaving Fort Laramie, the wagon train labored up and down the slopes of the Black Hills, where sweet-scented herbs and pungent sage permeated the air. Mountain cherry, currants, and tangles of wild roses lay against brushstrokes of blue flax, larkspur, and tulips. Game was prevalent, and solitary buffalo bulls roamed the ravines of terrain so rough it tested even the most recent wagon repairs, to say nothing of the most rested soul. Trudging a little off to one side while Sarah Jane took a turn driving, Amanda observed for the first time how rickety most of the rigs appeared. Even their own prairie schooner, once so new and sleek against the more clumsy Conestogas, showed the same deterioration. Hardly a wheel in the company was without a wedge or two hammered between it and the rim to fill gaps in the shrinking wood. Canvas tops above the rattling, creaking wagons were stained with grease and dust and bore patches or gaping holes from hail and wind. Animals that had begun the journey hale and hearty now appeared jaded and bony. . .and ahead lay even rougher country. So many, many miles yet to cover.

"Mandy?" Sarah barely paused. "What do you think of Alvin?"

"He's quite nice looking," Amanda fudged, then ventured further. "He has very gentlemanly manners, shows definite artistic talent, and will be quite rich someday, from what you've told me."

"Yes. That's true. All of it."

"Why do you ask?" With sadness Amanda skirted a child's

rocking horse that had been discarded by someone up ahead.

"I was just wondering."

"Has he. . .I mean, has he done something. . .ungentlemanly?"

Sarah shook her head. "No. But he's beginning to care. For me." Her voice vibrated with the jouncing of the seat.

The news did not come as much of a surprise, considering all the time the two had spent in each other's company. Glancing at her sister, Amanda expected to see a hint of excitement—even happiness—in her expression, yet Sarah seemed glum. Amanda could only pray that her sibling's trust in men would not be shattered as her own had been. "What about you, Sissy?"

Sarah's gaze drifted away, and she smiled. "He does meet a lot of the qualifications I set out when we first started this journey, doesn't he? He is rich. He is quite handsome."

"But?"

The smile wilted.

"I couldn't help but notice you seemed to be avoiding him, at Fort Laramie, while you spent more time with Bethany and Tad."

"I. . .needed time. To think."

Amanda could see her sister's unrest. "Tonight at camp we'll pray about things. Together, like we used to. Would you like that?"

Sarah only nodded.

&

After Amanda fell asleep, Sarah Jane eased off the pallet. The sudden absence of its comforting warmth became even more apparent as the chill of night crept around her. Shivering, she shook out an extra blanket and wrapped it about herself, lit a small candle, and opened her journal.

> *Dear Diary,*
> *It's been days and days since last I visited with*

*you. The rest at Fort Laramie did wonders for both
people and animals. A hard rain made the river too
swift to cross, so our departure was delayed an extra
day. The upper crossing of the North Platte, however, was without mishap, thanks to the Mormon
ferry. . .eight dugout canoes with logs laid across the
tops—an effective, if flimsy, method of transport.*

*Now, heading into the mountains, the land is
bleak and barren. Things that appear green in the
distance turn out to be only dry sand and rock,
sprinkled with stunted clumps of sage and grease-
wood.*

*It makes me sad whenever we pass castoff trea-
sures along the trail, but folks are trying to ease the
burden on the animals lumbering so earnestly in this
upward climb. We've been examining our own meager stores, wondering what we might be able to do
without, should our mules begin to falter.*

*I pray we all make it through this rough section of
country, so full of ravines and treacherous slopes.
Progress sometimes slows to a point that tempers
flare at the least provocation, and the men remain on
their guard for rattlesnakes and other wild animals.*

Tapping her pencil against her chin in thought, Sarah
frowned. Then after a short pause she continued writing.

*Alvin has expressed a desire for some kind of
commitment from me, but I've managed to put him
off, suggesting we remain friends for a while longer.
I always thought wealth was important, along with
one's outward appearance. . .But now such things
seem trivial. Especially in the face of true loss and
real struggle, like poor Bethy and Tad endure every
day. I feel a little guilty about hiding behind those*

little ones, though, while I try to decipher my true
feelings regarding Alvin. Mr. Hill seems greatly
appreciative of any thoughtfulness shown to his
children. He's quite a sensitive man—and ever so
much more mature than Alvin. I—

She stopped writing and nibbled at her lip, trying to put her feelings on paper. Then she erased the last word.

❧

Two of the hard days following the ferrying of the river were made all the more loathsome by scummy water, alkali springs, choking dust, and the putrid stench of animal carcasses lying in gruesome little pools of poisonous water. Then came a hideous stretch of deformed rock strata that tore relentlessly at hooves, boots, and wheels.

Finally, to everyone's relief, the valley of the Sweetwater River came in sight, with its easier grades, fine water, and grass to be enjoyed for more than a week's travel. Cheers again rang out when the huge bulk of Independence Rock loomed on the distant horizon.

"We'll be there to celebrate July fourth, Mandy," Sarah Jane exclaimed. "Right on time."

Amanda nodded. No one appreciated rest days more than she. Of all the recent tortures—steaming marshes, odorous sulphur springs, and the like—most horrendous had been the huge crawling crickets that crunched sickeningly beneath wheels and boots for a seemingly endless stretch of miles. Each day took increased effort to remain optimistic for Sarah's sake, while inwardly her feelings were anything but pleasant. Surmising that other women appeared to have things so much easier than she, with men to drive the wagons and look after repairs and animals, Amanda gritted her teeth, fighting feelings of jealousy and self-pity.

". . .so I said to him—" Sarah stepped closer to the wagon. "You're not even listening to me, are you?"

"Hm?"

"Oh, never mind. Do you feel all right, Mandy? You look flushed."

"I'm fine. Fine!" At her own uncharacteristic outburst, Amanda watched the scenery blur behind a curtain of tears.

"No, you're not. You're not fine at all."

Even Sarah's voice sounded faint, sort of fuzzy as she scrambled aboard. "You need to go lie down in back. I'll take over."

You can't. I'm the oldest. The one in charge. But the words wouldn't come out. In a wave of dizziness, Amanda relinquished the reins without a fuss and nearly toppled off the seat. She crawled back to the pallet. The rumble and rattle of the wheels made her head pound and pound. . .

Voices. Everywhere. Loud and laughing. Noise. Too much noise. And it was hot, so hot. . .or cold. How could one shiver so much when it was hot? Why couldn't the world just stop and be still. There had to be quiet somewhere. Where was Oregon? All a body really needed was peace and quiet, a place to rest. To sleep.

&

"Do you think she'll be all right?" Sarah looked anxiously to Mrs. Randolph, hating the waver in her own voice as she peered down again at Amanda's flushed face. At least her sister had stopped thrashing about and now appeared to be sleeping peacefully.

"Right as rain, soon enough," came the soothing reply. "Poor child's plumb exhausted, that's what. She's been workin' herself near to death, always doin', doin', never takin' time to be young."

"It's my fault," Sarah moaned miserably. "I've let her carry the whole load this entire journey. Now I'm being punished. What if—"

"Don't even think such nonsense," the older woman chided. She removed the wet cloth from Amanda's brow and rinsed it out in cool water before replacing it again. "Your sister's a person who takes responsibility serious, is all. She likes makin' it easy for you, seein' you having fun with the others. It makes her happy."

The truth of the statement only made Sarah feel worse. "And I was only too glad to run off and leave everything to her—even after declaring I'd help out more. I hate myself."

"Now, now." Mrs. Randolph patted Sarah's arm. "These days of rest here at Independence Rock will do her a world of good, you'll see. And when we're on the road again, she'll perk right up, wantin' to take over. See if she don't."

"I hope you're right. Mandy's all I've got left in this world. I'm sure not about to give her up!"

"Well, I'll be bringin' some broth by in a little while. See if you can get her to take some." With a nod, their kindly neighbor took her leave.

Sarah took Amanda's limp hand in hers and softly massaged it, praying she would open her eyes, be herself again . . .her dear strong Mandy, who was everything she wished to be herself. Confident, independent, capable. . .A rush of tears threatened to spill over, until a shuffling at the rear of the wagon brought her emotions back in check.

A voice cleared, and a familiar face peered through the back opening. "How's the patient?"

"Doing better, Mr. Holloway," Sarah answered. "Resting comfortably now."

He nodded and his expression appeared to relax. "Well, if you need anything, let me know."

"Thank you. That's very kind. I will."

More visitors came by throughout the day, one by one. Jared Hill, Alvin, Ma Pruett, all of them speaking in quiet voices.

Even Bethany tapped gently on the side of the wagon, her smudged face scrunched with concern. "I brought Miss Amanda some flowers," she whispered, clutching a raggedy bouquet in her hands. The stems were too short to put in water.

Sarah accepted the offering with a gracious smile. "Thank

you, sweetheart. She'll just love them when she wakes up."

"Papa said I can't stay, so I'd best go now."

Sending her off with a hug, Sarah felt comforted and hopeful. Maybe she and Mandy had a family after all, one given to them by God. She bowed her head in a prayer of thanks.

&

"So I missed the whole celebration," Amanda said in amazement as the train meandered past the spectacular slash in the granite mountains known as Devil's Gate, heading toward Split Rock and the much anticipated Ice Slough folks were eager to see, still a few days hence.

At the reins, her sister nodded. "Fireworks, gunshots, the raising of the flag, everything! I'd have thought the racket would have disturbed you."

"I never heard it. Any of it! Sorry I was such a bother."

"You weren't. You earned that rest—I'm just sorry you had to get sick to get it!"

"Well, I'm better now. Did you get to climb the rock, at least?"

Sarah's smile held a hint of guilt. "Actually, when I saw you were doing all right, I did go up with some of the others while Mrs. Randolph stayed with you. Alvin took a pot of axle grease along and wrote his name and mine together for all the world to see. Do you believe that?" She giggled. "When he went with Jason to catch the view from the far side, I added a few other names to the list. By the time we left to come back down, the list read, 'Jason and Alvin and Sarah Jane and Amanda and Mary Katharine, Bethany, and Tad.' Alvin never noticed."

Amanda couldn't help laughing. She adjusted her shawl over her warm coat as they rode in mountain air crisp with pine and the sweet perfume of wildflowers. Tomorrow she would either walk or drive, to spare the mules, but today it did feel good to ride—even on the hard, springless seat. She just wished she hadn't missed the festivities at Independence Rock.

"You sure had a lot of visitors while you were sick."

"Oh?"

Sarah guided the team around a fallen log. "Mrs. Randolph, of course, was a godsend. She was the one who knew it wasn't cholera, just exhaustion, and was a great encouragement to me. She made you that good broth."

"Sounds just like her. She's a dear."

"And then Jared Hill came, and Alvin, and Ma Pruett. Bethy picked the sweetest flowers and brought them to you. Even the wagon master checked on you."

Amanda's heart tripped over itself. "Mr. Holloway?"

"Mm-hmm. Told me to let him know if we needed anything. I know you think he's domineering and stodgy, but I found him to be rather. . .nice."

"Well, I suppose everyone has his good points," Amanda hedged. The man probably kept tabs on everyone in his train. Yes, that had to be it. Of course, chances were he'd come to see if the problem was cholera, even yet hoping to force her and Sarah to stay behind!

But, on the other hand, there was no harm in allowing a tiny part of her to dream he truly cared. . .as long as she didn't voice the thought aloud. No one needed to know such a seemingly inconsequential gesture would be locked inside the treasurehouse of her heart forever. After all, someone destined for spinsterhood could probably use a few secret dreams to look back on in later lonely years. Pretending to adjust her bonnet during an elaborate stretch, Amanda turned to see if the wagon master was anywhere within sight.

❧

Seth nudged his mount over a knoll, keeping an eye on the straggling cattle that plodded in the wake of the wagon train. Not many head had been lost up to this point. Not many travelers, either, considering how quickly and effectively an outbreak of cholera could wipe out an entire company. They'd been pretty lucky so far.

He'd noticed Amanda Shelby was up and about, too, after wearing herself out. Not that he cared, particularly, but someone with her spirit deserved a quick recovery, and he was glad the Almighty saw fit to give her one.

Strange, how he'd started attributing occasional circumstances to God's hand of late. Gramps would like that. Could he be smiling down from the pearly gates now? Next thing, Seth would find himself going back to praying on a regular basis, dusting off the little black Bible he'd kept out of Gramps' possessions. Wouldn't that be something. He smirked, hardly bothered by the fact that the concept no longer seemed so unthinkable. He must be getting old.

Shifting in his saddle, Seth felt the letter he'd gotten at the fort crinkle in the pocket of his trousers. He compressed his lips. So Liza wanted him back. The gall of that woman! After worming her way into his younger brother's life for no other reason than to spite Seth, she'd seen the error of her ways and wanted to call it quits. As if he'd go behind Drew's back like that! He grimaced and shook his head.

Time to get rid of that fool thing before Red came across it. Removing the papers from his pocket, Seth tore them to shreds and let the wind scatter the pieces far and wide.

Women. There sure was a shortage of truly honest and decent ones. Ones with real spirit who could bring out the best in a man, make him want to settle down.

When a certain feminine face and form drifted across his consciousness, Seth wasn't quite so quick to squelch the green-eyed vision. . .even though he figured he had a lot of good years left to boss trails while he saved up for that thoroughbred horse ranch he'd always dreamed of.

Urging Sagebrush after a cow that was too far off the trail, Seth spotted a familiar-looking cloth item on the ground and swung down to pick it up.

sixteen

Just before going over the sloping shoulder of the mountains, the girls paused for a last glance backward in the sage-scented morning, memorizing a scene they were unlikely ever to see again. The shining Sweetwater River, after its tempestuous roar through Devil's Gap, meandered lazily beneath a lucid aquamarine sky. Independence Rock looked like a slumbering turtle in the vast expanse of dry sage, and on the eastern horizon, misty hills discreetly hid their cache of new graves.

The trail ascending into the Rockies was lined with crusted snowbanks soiled with mud, twigs, and animal tracks. The route grew increasingly rough and rugged, some portions necessitating the use of chains and double teams to drag wagons one at a time up the steep grades. The temperature, too, reached new extremes. In the pleasant sunshine, rivulets of melted ice would trickle downhill to water sporadic patches of green starred with brilliant yellow flowers and clumped with iris. But at night, folks shivered around the insufficient sagebrush fires, longing for some of the spare blankets only recently discarded.

Hard days later they crested the summit, where massive clouds churned threateningly across the curved sky. Early snow dusted the range to the north. Sarah hunkered down into the turned-up collar of her coat and frowned at her sister as Amanda drove onward. "Isn't this where we're supposed to cross the Great Divide?" she hollered above the howling wind. "Somehow, I expected to see a dramatic gorge, or something spectacular—but it's only a grassy meadow!" She perused the wide, bumpy plain between two solid walls of impassible mountains.

"My thoughts exactly." Amanda grinned as a gust flailed her scarf. Then she sobered. "They say Doctor Marcus Whitman knelt with a flag and a Bible and prayed over the West on his first trip through this pass, before he ever set up the mission where he and his wife ministered to the Cayuse Indians."

Sarah pondered the tragic end of the courageous missionaries a moment before turning to a cheerier thought. "Well, at least the place isn't as rough and rugged as the route we had to take to get here. But I still would have expected some unforgettable landmark to indicate the crossing of the *Great Divide!*"

Amanda nodded in agreement.

The train rolled steadily through South Pass, then began the downward grade to the west. They paused at a spring for an icy ceremonial toast from the westward flowing water, then continued down to camp beneath the willows at Little Sandy Creek.

After supper, Sarah Jane left Amanda working on sewing projects and headed toward the Hill wagon.

Bethany and Tad came running the minute they saw her.

"Look at the pretty flowers I picked, Miss Sarah," Bethany said, proudly displaying the colorful wildflowers in her hand.

"And I found a real nice stone." Tad held out his open palm. "Pa says I can keep it, too."

Sarah smiled. "That's nice. I'm happy for both of you." Their father laid aside the worn harness he was examining and stood. "Mind keeping an eye on my pair while I go talk to your sister?" he asked.

Meeting his gaze, Sarah felt the color heighten in her cheeks. "Not at all. I'll take the children for a walk."

"Thanks. Much obliged." With that, he strode away.

Sarah wondered what he and Amanda would be discussing, then filled her lungs and exhaled. A person could have all kinds of things to talk about on an extended journey like this one. Maybe he was weary of having to look after their wagon in addition to his. Maybe he needed some mending done.

"Will you tell us a story, Miss Sarah?" Bethy's huge blue eyes rounded as she gazed raptly up at her.

"A scary one," Tad chimed in. "With dragons and sailing ships and—"

His sister pouted. "No. One with princesses and castles."

Sarah Jane wrapped an arm around each of them and gave a light squeeze. "Tell you what. I'll tell you my very favorite Bible story, about Naaman the leper and his little slave girl."

"Oh, goody!" Bethany clapped. "I like that one, too!"

❧

Sewing the hem in a flannel baby gown, Amanda looked up as Jared came toward her. "Good evening," she said politely.

He removed his hat and inclined his head, then without waiting for an invitation, lowered himself to a corner of the blanket. His posture remained rigid. "Where is everybody?" she asked lightly, gazing hopefully past him for his brood.

"The kids, you mean? Sarah took them for a walk."

Amanda gave an understanding nod. Something was in the air, she could feel it. Taking up her sewing again, her fingers trembled unaccountably, and she pricked her finger.

He appeared nervous too, fiddling with the brim of his hat, not quite meeting her gaze. "Amanda, I. . .have something to ask you," he began.

Now she was more than a little uneasy. "Something wrong with one of the children?" she asked, trying to steer the conversation in a safe direction.

"No, no. Nothing like that. Nothing like that at all."

"Oh, well, have we been making pests of ourselves, then? Sarah and I? Taking up too much of their time?"

He let out a slow breath. "This has nothing to do with Tad or Beth. Well, actually it does, sort of."

"I don't understand." Alarm bells were clanging in earnest inside Amanda's head. *Please, please, don't let it be what I think it is,* she prayed silently even as her heart began to throb with dread. Laying aside her project, she expended the enormous amount of effort required to look directly at him.

"This'll probably come as a shock, but I want you to hear me out. Don't say a word till I'm done."

"But—"

Jared's straight brows dipped slightly, silencing her. He cleared his throat and looked around. Then his eyes met hers. "I don't have to tell you how hard it's been on my kids—and me—losing their mother."

"I understand, but—"

This time a pleading look cut her off. "I came pretty near changing my mind about heading west, when she died. But there was nothing to go back to."

Feeling a shiver course through her, Amanda held her hands out to the warmth of the fire a few feet away.

"Gave more thought to dropping out when it seemed the trip was gonna be too hard on the young'uns. But then you and your sister stepped in." He shrugged. "Now they're normal kids again. Happy, enthusiastic about living out west. And you know what? So am I."

"Jared—"

"Not till I'm done, remember? I might never have enough gumption to bring this up again."

Amanda clamped her lips together.

"What I'm trying to say is, the kids and I would be mighty pleased if you were to go with us to wherever we settle. It's not right for them to grow up without a ma. I'd marry you, of course, make no mistake about that. And I'd be good to you, Amanda. Real good. I think the world of you, and so do my little ones."

Her mouth parted, whether in shock or dismay, she really wasn't sure. But her heart truly went out to Jared Hill. No one had to tell her he was a kind man, a sensitive and caring father. And she felt instinctively that he'd make a wonderful husband, too. . .if a woman were so inclined.

He tipped his head self-consciously. "Oh, I know I'm not much to look at. You could do lots better than me, that's for sure."

Amanda reached over with her hand and covered one of his, stilling its assault on the poor hat. "You, Jared Hill, are one of the nicest, most decent men I have ever met in my entire life. And you've done twice as much for us as we've ever done for you."

He smiled wryly. "Pretty sure I hear a but coming."

"Not for the reason you think," she admitted, then rattled off the first thing that came to her head. "It isn't you. It's me. I already have my future all planned out. . .and it doesn't include marriage—to anyone. There are things I want to do, on my own. And there's Sarah to consider. I'm the only family she has."

"But your sister's welcome to come with us, too," he insisted. "We'd both look after her until she found someone she wanted to spend her life with. You wouldn't have to worry about her at all."

Amanda hesitated.

Jared filled the silence. "Well, it'd be enough if you'd just think on it. Would you do that? Who knows, maybe by the time we go the rest of the way to Oregon you might change your mind."

"I wouldn't count on it," she answered in what she sincerely hoped was a kind tone. "It's not fair for you to get your hopes up too high."

"Then, I won't. But just know the offer stands. I'll not beat you over the head with it. It's up to you."

"Thank you, Jared. I really mean that. It's the kindest, nicest offer I've had in my life."

He grinned, a touch of embarrassment tugging it off center. "I might have figured you'd had others."

"Only one. One too many," she confessed bitterly.

His expression softened into one of understanding. "Must

have been a dimwit to let a fine woman like you slip away."
His face grew solemn and he cleared his throat once more,
then ambled to his feet. "Well, I'd be obliged if you just gave
the matter some thought. It's all I ask."

Amanda got up also. "I will. Truly. But—"

"I know." With a cockeyed smile, Jared turned and went
back in the direction of his wagon.

A host of conflicting emotions made her watch after him
until he was out of sight.

That night, when the majority of folks gathered around the
campfire for a hymn sing, Amanda remained behind. Taking
down the empty wooden pail outside her wagon, she glanced
toward the gathering. Hardships of the journey showed on
everyone, clothing ragged and worn hung loosely on the thin-
ner forms, but the faces aglow with the golden light of the big
fire looked peaceful. It was no surprise to hear "Abide With
Me" issue forth soon after the singing began. Smiling, she
drew away and strolled the short distance to the stream.

The quiet, gurgling brook had been pretty in the fading
light of day, but now in the growing darkness it surpassed its
former beauty as the ripples spilled over rocks in the stream
bed, catching remnants of firelight in shining ribbons of silver
and gold. Amanda set down the bucket. Stooping near the
edge, she trailed her fingers in the cold current, then licked
her fingertips, enjoying the sweetness of pure water after so
many bitter and cloudy springs.

"Nice crisp evening," a low voice said quietly.

Amanda sprang to her feet.

Several yards away, the wagon master stood after filling
and capping his canteen. He thumbed the brim of his hat in a
polite gesture.

"Mr. Holloway." She returned her attention to the creek as,
to her dismay, the rate of her pulse increased.

"You don't cotton to singing?"

Her hands slid into her coat pockets in an effort to remain

casual. "Normally I would. Just not tonight."

From the corner of her eye, she saw him nod slightly. "I was glad to see you back on your feet so soon after being sick."

Slowly raising her lashes, she peered toward him. Warmth coursed through her, almost making the cool, fall evening feel more like a midsummer night. She swallowed. "I heard you'd come by. Thank you for the concern."

His dark eyes were completely lost in the shadow of his hat brim, but Amanda could feel the intensity of his fixed gaze. "I like to make sure my company stays healthy."

Amanda didn't respond.

"You've been kind of a surprise—or rather, amazement—to me," the man went on. "Never thought you'd stick out the hardships of the trip."

"I hope you didn't lose any bets over it," she blurted, immediately hating herself.

But he chuckled.

Amanda felt compelled to smooth over the hasty remark. "We're thankful God has brought us this far."

With a soft huff, he started toward her. "You're really serious about giving the Almighty all the credit, even though you're the one doing all the work?"

Sensing that he was baiting her, Amanda frowned. It seemed immensely important for the wagon master to understand her simple logic, her simple faith. "He gives us strength to do it."

"I suppose." Closer now, he picked up the pail and dipped it into the stream, filling it to the brim, then set it next to her on the grass.

Her surprise over the act of kindness almost clouded over the realization that he hadn't made light of her convictions this time.

Mr. Holloway continued to stare. "Oh." He reached into an inside pocket of his buckskin jacket and drew out a calico bonnet. "I believe this belongs to you."

"Y-yes," she gasped. "It does. I lost it a few days ago." Taking the article from him, her fingers brushed his calloused hand, and a maddening blush flamed her face. It intensified with the awareness that the cloth retained the heat of his body. She knew better than to trust her voice. "Thank you," she could only whisper.

He nearly smiled. "Wouldn't want you coming down with something else, now, would we?" he teased.

Amanda's lips parted in disbelief at this glimpse of yet another aspect of his personality. He was far more complex than she'd given him credit for. . .and perhaps, far more *fascinating*. Realizing the dangerous turn her imaginings were taking, Amanda became aware that she was gawking at the man and clamped her mouth closed.

"Well, I wouldn't stay out here too long, Miss Shelby. Night brings out all kinds of thirsty animals." He bent to pick up the water bucket, then motioned with his head for her to walk beside him.

"Do you—?" Both of them spoke at once.

Having paused at the same time as well, they smiled. He gestured for her to go first.

Amanda only shook her head. "Never mind." In an attempt to prolong the conversation she was on the verge of making some inane query regarding the trail. She was more curious as to what he had to say.

"I. . .don't suppose you like horses."

Completely taken by surprise, she turned her gaze fully on him. "I—they're beautiful creatures. I've never had one of my own, of course, but who wouldn't think they're wonderful animals?"

He showed no visible reaction. They had reached her wagon. Setting the pail up on the schooner within her easy reach, he then assisted her up as well.

Conscious of the touch of his hands on her waist, Amanda had to remember to breathe as he lightly set her down. "Thank you, Mr. Holloway," she managed as, with a half smile, he walked away.

Inside the warmer confines of the bowed top, Amanda fought a peculiar assortment of giddy, fluttery sensations she had never before experienced. Left over from her bout with sickness, she rationalized. That was it. Surely her imaginings were getting the best of her. It was time to calm down.

When at last she had regained her composure, she thought again of the unexpected marriage proposal—more than likely the cause of all this confusion—and knelt in the honey-colored lantern light.

Dear Heavenly Father, I thank you for the opportunity to come to you in prayer. You've been so merciful to Sarah and me over the many miles we've traveled. You've looked after us, kept us from harm, and given us so many blessings, so many friends.

Surely You know of this new predicament I face. A proposal—after all the time I've spent convincing myself never to trust a man again, much less expect one to look upon me with favor. I don't think I've given Mr. Hill the slightest indication of my desiring to replace his dear dead wife. Nor have his actions toward me, to be truthful. More than likely he's thinking of his children, trying to do what's best for them.

She paused and sighed. *But I couldn't imagine committing myself to another man unless I truly, truly loved him. And the affection I feel for Jared is not of that nature. In fact, I—*

Refusing even to finish the stunning thought trying to come to life within her heart, Amanda steeled herself against it and returned to her petition with renewed urgency. *Please give me wisdom to make the right choice. Help me to do your will, to do what's best. In Jesus' name, Amen.*

Not exactly at peace, Amanda draped her coat over one of the barrels and slid into the warm quilts and blankets on the pallet.

But it was not Jared Hill's face that remained in her thoughts.

seventeen

While they camped at Little Sandy, a vote was taken to bypass Fort Bridger and navigate the shorter route to Bear Valley known as Sublett's Cutoff. The idea of saving eighty-five miles—even at the price of heading straight out into a grassless desert tableland—seemed of more import than the difficulties they knew would have to be faced. Every available water container was filled to the brim in the clear cool river before leaving, and the men cut a supply of long grass for the animals.

The thought of seven days' less travel appealed to Amanda, whatever the hardships. Considering all she and Sarah Jane had endured up to this point, she had no qualms about trusting the Lord to take them through a dry march as well.

The memory of Seth Holloway's unexpected kindness last evening had kept her awake long into the night, try as she might to slough it off as mere good-neighbor courtesy. The man was an enigma. Though usually displaying a hard, domineering side of his character, he also possessed a caring, thoughtful side. The latter caused Amanda the most unrest and was hardest to ignore.

And there was Jared Hill's proposal to consider. The more she thought about it, the more convinced she became that the needs of the motherless children were uppermost in the widower's mind. After all, a remote homestead in sparsely settled territory demanded the combined efforts of a man and a woman to provide a nurturing environment for little ones. And she truly loved Bethany and Tad as if they were her own younger brother and sister. . .yet—

"Mandy?" Sarah asked, keeping pace with the plodding mules. "Would you like me to drive? You look tired."

Amanda shook her head. "I'm fine, really. It was just kind of a short night." She paused, debating whether or not to seek her younger sister's advice. But who else was there to ask? "Sissy. . .what do you think of Mr. Hill?"

Sarah turned her head so abruptly she stumbled on the uneven terrain. "Why?"

"He. . .he's asked me to marry him." Amanda watched the color drain from her sister's face.

"D-do you love him?" she asked, her words barely audible over the hoof falls and the rattle and creak of the wagon.

Amanda averted her gaze to the countryside, still amazingly pleasant for all the dire predictions of what lay ahead. "I like and respect him very much. It would be hard to find a more decent man." Hearing no reply, she glanced at her sibling again.

Sarah moistened her lips. "Does he. . .love you?"

A ragged breath emptied Amanda's lungs. She tipped her head in thought. "We both love the children. I think that's what's most important to him at the moment."

"They are dear, aren't they? Truly dear." A wistful smile played over Sarah's lips.

Amanda thought she detected a mistiness in her sister's eyes before Sarah quickly cut a glance to the earth. But the tear her sibling brushed away while trying to hide the action was not imagined. "Are you all right, Sissy?"

Sarah merely nodded. But she did not speak another word for hours.

๛

Crossing the crucible of sand speckled with prickly creosote and mesquite shrubs, the temperature climbed with the merciless sun. The bone-weary emigrants decided to rest during the day under the meager shade of canvas or wagon and journey at night, to spare the animals. But at least half a dozen beasts perished anyway, dropping right where they stood in the extreme scorching temperatures. People began abandoning wagons and doubling what remained of their teams.

Days later, the sight of the Green River on the far western side couldn't have been more welcome. The animals practically stampeded toward the swift, deep water. When everyone's thirst had been sated, the necessary preparations began for transporting the company across the formidable river. Some people by now routinely unpacked their heavy wagons and floated their stores over the water on rafts, then had to repack everything once the empty wagons reached the other side.

Amanda, having successfully forded numerous rivers, decided to chance this one as well. She tied down everything and inched the team into the Green after one of the other rigs.

The mules balked at the force of the flow, but started toward the opposite bank, making slow but steady progress.

Part way across, a front wheel struck something and buckled. The wagon pitched sharply to the left.

With Sarah's scream still ringing in her ears, Amanda plunged headlong into the frigid mountain flow. The roiling water whisked her away, hiding any view of her sister or the wagon.

Helpless against the force of the current, she made a futile attempt to swim, but the weight of her sodden skirts pulled her under, tangling about her legs—and her shoes felt as heavy as anvils. With the icy river roaring over her head and shoulders, Amanda fought desperately to keep her face above the surface, but each time she gasped for air she swallowed more water. She had to try to make it to shallower water—but no amount of thrashing with her arms could overcome the force of the relentless current. And the cold mercilessly sapped her strength. *I'm going to drown!* The sick realization clenched her heart. What would become of poor Sarah! *Dear God,* she prayed desperately, *take care of her. Don't let anything happen to her.*

Suddenly something snagged her around the shoulders. Cut off her air.

Amanda writhed frantically to get free.

"Don't fight me!"

As the command penetrated her numbed mind, Amanda became aware of a strong arm encircling her. Exhausted, she gave in, aware only of a man's labored breathing as he attempted to get them both to shore.

Coughing water from her lungs, Amanda clung to her rescuer. She blinked to clear her vision, then raised her lashes—and discovered that the masculine body pressed to hers was the wagon master's! The two of them were being pulled toward the bank by a rope.

When Amanda's feet grazed the sandy bottom, she was scooped up and carried to dry land. Still coughing as Seth Holloway set her down and loosed her death grip from his neck, she shivered uncontrollably in the wind.

His partner quickly wrapped the blanket from behind his saddle around her, while Mr. Holloway, enshrouded in his own, mounted his horse. Then she was lifted again into the wagon master's arms, and he started back toward the crossing site.

Deep shudders racked Amanda as the horse plodded along. She relived the ordeal as if it were a dream that hadn't ended yet—and she wondered if she would ever again in her life feel warm enough. Gathering the pitiful remnants of her remaining energy, she tried to speak over her violent shivers as they jounced along. Nothing would come out. "S-Sarah," she finally managed between chatters of her teeth.

"The others are probably looking after her."

"Y-you s-saved my life. Th-thank you."

An angry whoosh deflated his chest. "You almost got us both killed!" he ranted. "You had no business driving that wagon across by yourself. But you're bound and determined to prove me wrong." With another furious huff he shook his head. "I swear, you've been nothing but trouble from the first time I saw you!"

Utterly crushed by the attack, Amanda felt welling tears, but she had no time to respond. They had arrived at camp.

"Mandy!" Sarah ran up and yanked her to the ground in a bone-crushing hug. "Thank heaven you're all right!"

"Poor thing's near froze to death," she heard Mrs. Randolph say as another blanket was thrown about her. "Bring her over by the fire. Give a hustle, now. We have some good strong coffee on to help warm her up."

Amanda allowed them to lead her to the blazing campfire. Glancing over her shoulder, she saw Seth Holloway headed in the opposite direction. But she was far too spent to give further thought to her reluctant rescuer or his insulting tongue-lashing.

Shielded from view by a wall of blankets and concerned women, Sarah Jane stripped Amanda's sodden clothing from her stiff, shivering frame. Then layers of dry covers and quilts wrapped her from head to toe, providing the first measure of real warmth she'd felt since being drawn from the frigid river.

Much sooner than she would have expected, the ministrations of her sister and the kind older woman who'd become such a friend to them began thawing her out. With her stiff fingers wrapped around a hot mug, Amanda drained the last drop of coffee, then asked the question foremost in her mind. "When can I go lie down in the wagon?"

Sarah paled. "That's the bad news. But the men were able to salvage most of our things, and Mr. Hill is trying to fashion a cart for us from what's left of the schooner. When it tipped, he and another man came to help me. They saved the mules, too. Poor things were scared silly, braying their heads off."

"But don't you worry none, darlin'," Mrs. Randolph said gently. "You and Sarah Jane can sleep under our rig every night. We'll look after you."

Still stunned by the dire fate of the prairie schooner, Amanda drew little comfort from her neighbor's offer. Her expression must have been transparent, for Sarah Jane swiftly took command of the conversation, saying more all at once than she'd said for days. "Your heroic rescue was the talk of the camp, Mandy," she announced much too brightly.

Amanda just stared at her.

Her sister nodded. "Everyone gasped when that wheel snapped and you were flung into the river. Mr. Holloway had already crossed with the herd and was riding along the bank when you fell in. You should have seen him!" Sarah's eyes grew large. "He yelled something to that Mr. Hanfield and charged after you. Honestly, if ever a real true knight existed, that man fits the bill. It was almost. . .romantic." A smile gave emphasis to her airy sigh.

But Amanda felt tears gathering inside her soul. All she wanted was to be alone so she could cry her heart out. And she knew it had nothing to do with her harrowing experience.

❧

Having merged from the cutoff onto the rugged hills of the main trail once more, Amanda truly appreciated the way the much smaller cart handled. It wasn't exactly as stylish as something back east, but considering the poor shape of the materials used to make it, it rolled over the high ridges and through the pine forests as well—if not better—than many of the heavy wagons. Best of all, hitched to only four mules rather than six, it gave the animals an easier lot, too. Amanda could rotate them. And Jared Hill had thoughtfully made a canvas cover, which provided at least some shelter, in a pinch.

She had not seen Mr. Holloway since the incident at the Green River. Nor did she intend to see or speak to him for the remainder of the journey. Sarah, too, she noticed, had reverted to that oddly quiet way she'd acquired of late. She rarely spent time with Alvin or his friends, and even her moments with Bethany and Tad seemed weighted by her countenance.

Jared Hill had insisted the girls drive in front of him so he could keep an eye on their tentative conveyance, so the children normally walked beside either her or Sarah Jane, whichever one of them was afoot. Their endless chatter kept Amanda's mind occupied—another of life's blessings—while yet another ten, twenty, fifty miles ticked by. Would this tedious journey never end? Points of interest they passed along the way no longer held the slightest appeal, not even the amazing springs where the water tasted like soda.

Lost in moody depression, one afternoon, Amanda thought she imagined a cry in the distance. She peered ahead at a tiny cloud of dust that appeared to be coming toward them.

The shout came again.

"Gold!"

And again. *"Gold!"*

Much clearer now. Folks up front hollered it back to the rest and halted their teams.

Upon reaching the company, the galloping rider skidded his mount to a stop. "There's gold in California!" he yelled for all to hear, panting between breaths. "At Sutter's Mill, on the American River. Enough for all! I'm ridin' east to fetch my brothers." With that, he spurred his lathered horse and sped on.

A moment of silent shock swiftly evolved into an excited murmur, then erupted to hoots and howls.

"Well, I, for one, am headin' to Californy," one man bellowed. "Soon as we pass the fort!" Waving his hat, he kicked up his heels and jumped aboard his outfit, clucking his team to motion.

"Me, too," another hollered.

A virtual shouting match broke out down the line, between folks bound and determined to grab this chance to get rich, and others who declared they were continuing to Oregon despite what could turn out to be a rumor started by some practical joker.

Just listening to the melee, Amanda and Sarah exchanged questioning frowns.

Then Mr. Holloway cantered by, one hand raised, on his way to the front of the line. "Let's not get all het up, folks," he said a number of times. "Stay calm. Whether there's gold or not, there's plenty of time for you and your animals to rest up at the fort while you think the matter through. Then if you decide to turn off on the California Trail when we come to it, at least you'll have a better chance of getting there in one piece."

But there was no slowing down some of the determined travelers. Breaking off from the rest of the train, those wagons pulled ahead, anxious to set out on fortune's path.

A much smaller group made camp that night.

Amanda felt exposed as she and Sarah were forced to sleep out in the open. Listening to plaintiff yips and howls of coyotes and wolves, the rustlings in the sagebrush that could be any number of wild things, she rolled up in her blanket like a mummy and lay awake waiting for utter exhaustion to claim her.

All she wanted was to get somewhere. *Anywhere.* Never to go another mile again. Someplace where she never had to set eyes on Seth Holloway as long as she lived. As they had for the past several nights, burning tears slid out from behind her closed eyes and into her hair.

eighteen

From a distance of five miles the whitewashed fur-trading post of Fort Hall was visible, occupying half an acre of sagebrush plain alongside the shining Snake River. The breeze played over the red flag on the pole, ruffling the initials of the Hudson's Bay Company. But this time upon approaching a fort, the mood of the company was a peculiar mixture of excitement and subdued resignation.

Amanda gave no more than a cursory glance to the five-foot wall surrounding the two-story bastion or the hewn log buildings inside. Word had it there was no meat, flour, or rice to be had. Only a small supply of coffee and sugar—and that at fifty cents a pint. Nevertheless, two days of rest would be appreciated. "Look, Pa!" she heard Tad shout. "A cannon! A real cannon!"

But before the lad could skip off to the piece of artillery parked in the courtyard, his father reined him in. "Slow down, son. That's nothing to fool with."

The boy groaned in disappointment.

Jared tousled the towhead's hair on his approach to Amanda and Sarah. "If you two would look after the young'uns, I'd like to go hunting with the other men. See if I can replenish our stores."

Amanda nodded. "Go on. I'll see to your oxen."

With a grateful smile at her and Sarah, he retrieved his rifle and walked toward the loose horses among the animals that had trailed the company. Amanda thought she caught a wistful longing in her sister's expression as he left.

"I'm hungry, Miss Sarah," Bethany implored.

Her brother perked up. "Me, too."

"Well, let's see what we can scrape together," Amanda heard her say, "while Sissy takes care of the animals."

 za

That night, the camp was anything but quiet. News of the gold strike had the whole place abuzz, precluding the customary music and dancing while folks made plans for the remainder of the journey. Amanda and Sarah sipped coffee by their evening fire until Jared tucked his little ones into bed.

Moments after he came to join them, the Randolphs paid a visit as well. Beaming from ear to ear, the older couple had a stranger in tow. It took Amanda only one look to guess the young man was their son. He bore an uncanny resemblance to his father, already possessing similar body structure and bearing, and the same pear-shaped face. But one striking difference stood out—he had the brightest red hair Amanda had ever seen.

"We'd like you all to meet our Charlie," Minnie Randolph said proudly, her small blue eyes aglow as they rested on him. "He's just come over from California to meet his pa an' me. Charlie, this is Amanda—the sweetest little gal a body could know—and her sister Sarah Jane, and Jared Hill, our neighbor." She indicated each in turn.

Amanda blushed at the emphasis of her name.

"Howdy," he managed, fair sunburnt skin turning an even deeper hue up to his hairline as he nodded to her, then Sarah. He shook hands with Jared, who had risen to his feet.

"How'd you find the desert trail?" Jared asked.

"Not much good a person can say about that," the young man admitted candidly. "But I figured my folks would do all right with me to help out."

"Would any of you care for some coffee?" Amanda asked, regaining her composure as Sarah spread out an extra blanket.

"Don't mind if we do," the elder Mr. Randolph said, kneading his bearded jaw. He assisted his wife, then settled his solid bulk between her and their son as they accepted the proffered refreshment.

"Mm. Tastes mighty good," the old man commented. "Near as good as Minnie's, if I do say so."

His spouse beamed in agreement. "Reason we come by," she said, centering her attention on Amanda, "is to invite you an' your sister to come to California with us when we take the cutoff."

Aware of the woman's son on the fringe of her vision, Amanda blanched. "We—"

She held up a gnarled hand. "I know, the store an' all. But seems like the Good Lord's layin' a real good chance at your feet. You won't know a soul when you get to Oregon, and more'n likely, folks who've suffered the hot sands and dry waste of the desert will be needin' clothes as much as anybody else. Might be, you could even happen across a few nuggets of gold to help get you started. We'll be passin' nigh Sutter's Fort on the way to our new place, a handful of miles farther."

"I've been considering heading off on that fork myself," Jared announced out of the blue before Amanda had opportunity to reply. "I was gonna make you and Sarah Jane the same offer."

Sarah, raising her mug to her lips, halted midway and lowered it to her lap instead.

Amanda had never once considered branching off the main trail and settling in California. Her sights had been fixed on Oregon since before leaving Independence. She looked to Sarah for a response and found her sister's expression unreadable as the younger girl stared at Alvin Rivers' wagon.

"My other offer still stands, too," Jared told Amanda quietly when the others began talking among themselves.

It was all too much to take in at once. Amanda felt torn in two. Either route had definite merit as well as dreaded pitfalls. But she wasn't exactly up to committing her entire future in marriage just yet, either. Looking to her sibling once more, her gaze drifted above Sarah's shoulder and happened upon Seth Holloway, exiting the fort's general store with his partner. That same instant, his attention flicked her way. He tipped his head slightly in Amanda's direction and said something to Mr. Hanfield. They both laughed.

Amanda set her jaw. One good thing about the Lord, she reasoned, He always provides a way of escape, just as He promised in First Corinthians. With a glance encompassing the Randolphs, Jared Hill, and her sister, she hiked her chin. "We'll do it. We'll go to California!"

❧

"You're not serious!" Alvin snapped his sketchpad closed in the only true display of his temper Sarah had ever witnessed. His charcoal pencil and blending stick fell unheeded to the sandy ground outside the fort, where he'd been working on a new landscape.

"I'm afraid I am," she replied, shielding her eyes from the bright sun. "When the wagon train leaves this fort tomorrow morning, Mandy and I have decided to take the California Trail with the Randolphs, Mr. Hill, and whoever else will be splitting off from the company."

"But why would you do a fool thing like that?" Not to be put off, he sidled up to her, his fingertips lightly grazing up and down her forearm. "For—gold? I'm already in line for a considerable fortune, you know. I'm not about to waste weeks and months grubbing through a bunch of rocks and mud for a few paltry nuggets."

"I never suggested you should."

His movements halted. "I see." The light that dawned in his head was almost visible in his eyes and lent them a steely glitter. "So this is good-bye, then. Fare thee well and all that."

Sarah nodded, brushing aside a loose tendril the fall breeze whisked over her face. "I thought I'd tell you now, while there's still time to talk. But please don't think ill of me, Alvin.

I'll always remember you. I'll think back with pleasure on the happy times we shared on this journey. And I truly hope one day you'll find someone who'll fulfill all your dreams. She'll be a very fortunate person."

"Indeed." A smirk lifted a corner of his mouth. "I thought I already had."

"No." Slowly shaking her head, Sarah smiled thinly. "There was only room in your heart for me. My dream is to be part of a family. . .the bigger the better. To bear children and watch them grow and have children of their own. Even if I were poor and had to scratch for my existence I could never settle for less than that."

He raked long fingers through his wiry curls and shook his head. Then, reaching for both her hands, he pulled her into a warm hug, his heart beating against hers for several seconds until finally he eased her to arm's length. "Tell you one thing, Sarah Jane Shelby. If it were a few years down the line and I'd already been to all the places I plan to see, I just might be tempted to *settle for* a piece of that dream of yours. But not right now."

She smiled sadly.

Alvin paused and searched her face as though committing it to memory. Then he raised her chin with the edge of an index finger and lightly brushed her lips with his. "Well, do be happy. . .little *friend*. Any young lady who happens across my path in the future is sure going to have a lot to measure up to. Who knows, perhaps one day we'll meet again, and you'll be able to show me your brood of little ones."

Fighting tears, Sarah could only attempt to smile as she took his hand and squeezed it in mute silence. Then she turned away and walked slowly back to the gate.

≈

Amanda braced her heart against even a twinge of regret the next day as the cutoff to California loomed ever nearer. Ignoring an inner sense of guilt over not having prayed about her rash decision, she purposefully closed her mind to scenery and everyday matters and focused on the future, on the blessed time when she would no longer be forced to suffer the unbearable presence of wagon master Holloway. She determined not to even announce her change in plan to the man. Likely he would be relieved anyway that she and Sarah would no longer be his responsibility. And Amanda had no desire to provide another opportunity for him to gloat. Nor would she permit her gaze to seek him out during nooning stops or evening camps. Whatever strange fascination she might have felt toward the man, it was time it died a quick, natural death. So decided, she ceased the solitary evening walks she had previously enjoyed and expended the supreme effort required to center her attention within the three- or four-yard circumference around her person. After all, she had mules to tend, meals to cook and clean up. It would do well to get used to being with the lesser number of travelers who would be turning off at the split tomorrow.

That night at the campfire, Deacon Franklin prayed for those who on the morrow would part company with the remainder of the Oregon Trail travelers. Reflecting on his thoughtful words, afterward, Amanda finally willed herself to sleep. Morning dawned in grayness, and Amanda drew perverse pleasure that it matched her mood. After what seemed an interminable length of time to dispose of breakfast and early chores, the signal finally sounded to roll.

"This is it," Sarah breathed, her excitement barely concealed. With Bethany on one side of her and Tad on the other, she waved to their father and began walking at a brisk pace.

Amanda mustered all her resolve. Tonight, camped on a new trail, her heart would sing a victory song. She was sure of it. Refusing to acknowledge the silly tear that teetered over her lower lashes and plopped onto her hand, she clucked the team forward.

Riding at the rear end of the column, Seth watched the company dwindle as, one by one, wagons turned off onto the California Trail, taking along several head of cattle that they had cut out of the herd earlier this morning. Granted, some folks retained sense enough to continue on to Oregon Territory, but out of the nearly thirty families who had begun this journey at Independence three months ago, it appeared only a handful would stay with the original plan.

Oh well, he mused, it would make the job easier on him, Red, and the scouts. There were some pretty rugged mountains yet to be crossed. He shook his head. The hardships on this route were nothing compared to what lay ahead of those gold-crazy fools. His friend, Thomas Fitzpatrick, had related some amazing tales of overlanders he had bossed across that frying pan.

Only three wagons had yet to come to the branch. Seth watched the Randolphs turn off. He'd known from the onset their destination was to be northern California. He'd found Nelson Randolph a decent man, one who had acquired respect from a lot of the folks during this journey. Having a son come to meet them with the foresight to trail a string of extra mules and water, Seth figured the old couple would make out okay—provided the heat didn't do them in.

Nearby, a bony heifer meandered away from the fringe. Seth nudged his mount in that direction and brought the wanderer back in line.

He glanced ahead once more, and his heart lurched. The Shelby cart had veered onto the southerly trail toward the Raft River—with that widower, Hill, right behind!

A battle raged as Seth fought the irrational desire to chase after Amanda and spare her from the horrific dangers of that route. After all, he had somewhat enjoyed playing rescuer once. But on the other hand, he reminded himself, she was no longer his responsibility now—wasn't that what he'd wanted all along?

He shifted grimly in the saddle and watched the rickety cart growing smaller in the distance. Once Amanda crossed the river, she would be on her way to an entirely different world.

Leaving his own profoundly empty.

nineteen

Sarah Jane studied her sister as Amanda walked with the children along the blistered sagebrush trail. For days, ever since they had foregone their original plan and taken the California branch, Amanda had been moody and quiet. She seemed to be doing her best to be cheerful around Bethy and Tad and polite to Jared and the Randolphs. . .but she had changed drastically after her near drowning.

Before the incident Amanda had been her normal, jovial self most of the time. Even inwardly happy, as if she had come to terms with the shameful way Pa's dastardly partner had humiliated them all, before thoughts of heading west ever came up. For some time, now, there'd been nary a shred of the bitterness only Sarah could discern in her sibling's eyes. That close brush with death had disturbed Amanda far more deeply than she let on. With a deep sigh, Sarah sent a prayer aloft that God would bring her sister through this hard time.

That night she waited until Amanda's even breathing indicated sleep, then lit a candle and opened her journal to the next page.

Dear Diary,
In my worst imaginings, I never would have dreamed a more sterile, desolate region than is all around us on this California Trail. After crossing the river, we descended upon a landscape consisting entirely of burnt rocks and cinders. High, blackened cliffs towered above our camp the first night.
We found surprisingly good grass and water when

*we reached the Humboldt River, whose benefits we
enjoyed for nearly two weeks—but one day it disappeared into a most distressing alkali swamp, and we
left it behind to make our way across a vast sea of
hot sand.*

*The sun beats down upon us mercilessly, sucking
the very moisture from our bodies, while the wagon
wheels churn up an unbearable cloud of dust. It
coats man and beast alike from head to foot, filling
our nostrils and burning our eyes. How I yearn to
see another glorious waterfall like those we passed
after departing Fort Hall.*

A snore drifted her way from the confines of the Randolph
wagon. Sarah peeked around to see if the sound had roused
any of the others, then resumed her writing.

*We should reach the mountains tomorrow. We've
been looking at them for the past two days as they sat
on the horizon like a mirage. Hopefully there will be
water there—and grass for our poor, weary animals.*
Mandy and I both long to see the end of this journey.

A cool gust of night wind caused Sarah to shiver. Marveling
at the vacillating desert temperatures, she tucked the journal
away and snuggled deep into her covers.

❧

It was a delightful treat to camp beside a stream again, to have
actual shade and lush grasses. For one whole day, the company rested, bathed, and washed clothing in readiness for the
trek up the rugged mountain trail.

Amanda had never enjoyed a bath so much—even such a
cold one. After the tortures of the desert, she was beginning
to feel her spirit come to life again. It seemed the passing of
miles helped ease the ache in her heart as well, but she knew

it would take some time before it dissipated completely. . .if ever. Surely the worst of the journey must be over. Traipsing back toward the cart with some wet laundry draped over her arm, she saw Jared staring her way as he leaned against the trunk of a tree. "Jared," she said pleasantly.

"Amanda." He tossed a handful of pebbles aside that he'd been rolling around in his hand. "Mind if we talk a spell? Your sister's got the kids."

"Not at all." But a trickle of uneasiness crept along her spine. She carefully laid the clothes on the grass.

Jared sank to the ground and brushed a spot smooth for her, then offered a hand. "Give any more thought to the offer I made a while back?" he asked, his long face became serious as he came right to the point.

She chewed the inside corner of her lip and nodded.

"And?" he prompted.

Turning to him, Amanda let out a nervous breath. Loath as she was to hurt the man, leading him on would be ten times worse. "I cannot accept it," she said softly. "I'm truly sorry."

Jared stared at her for a timeless moment, then expelled a resigned breath as he looked off into the distance. "Figured as much."

"Somehow, I knew you might," she replied, "but I also knew you probably wouldn't understand my reasons."

He plucked a handful of grass and let the breeze take a few blades. "Mind if I ask what they are?"

"One of them, you might be surprised to hear, is love." At his perplexed expression, she went on. "I've grown to love you a lot, on this journey, Jared. . .but it isn't the right sort of love to build a life on."

"Sure about that?"

She nodded. "I told you once that I had no plans ever to marry, and that's truer now than the day I said it. You're an incredible, wonderful man. You deserve a wife who will love you with all her heart. . .and it wouldn't be fair for me to stand in her way."

Jared slowly filled his lungs, obviously mulling her words over in his mind. Averting his gaze once more, he cocked his head back and forth. "Well, I only asked you to consider it. I'll do my best to accept your decision. Even if I don't agree."

"One day you will," Amanda said with a smile. "You'll see."

≈

"It'd be a shame not to share some of these apple fritters," Amanda remarked, "after hording the last of our dried apples so long." She gathered several and wrapped them in a cloth.

Sarah tried to ignore a peculiar awkwardness within as her sister left her and Jared and crossed the small wagon circle toward the Randolphs, seated around their own evening fire. "You've gotten to be a mighty fine cook, Sarah Jane," the widower said, popping the final bite of his own fritter into his mouth. "You and Amanda both." He refilled his mug from the coffeepot and relaxed against the wheel of his Conestoga.

More than a little aware of Jared's presence and close proximity, the scant width of a blanket from her, Sarah Jane tried not to blush as her eyes met his. She wished she had courage enough to lose herself in their sad blue depths, but quickly looked away instead. "I think Sissy and I are more surprised than anyone! You would not believe the awful fare we had to choke down when we first started out on the trail. Of course," she rambled on in her nervousness, "we had a pretty good teacher in Mrs. Randolph. She's taught us a lot."

"Fine woman."

"Yes. A great friend. Mandy thinks the absolute world of her and her husband after all they've done for us. That's probably the main reason she wanted to share our dessert with them tonight."

He nodded, idly taking another gulp of the strong brew.

"Mr. Hill—"

"Jared," he corrected. "Fits better."

Sarah swallowed. "I know," she said breathlessly. "It's just that—Well—You're so much older than the boys I've been around all my life."

He gave her a pained look.

She wanted to crawl into a hole. "I—I don't mean you're old. Not at all."

A chuckle rumbled from deep inside his chest.

Drawing a huge breath to calm herself, Sarah tried again. "What I mean is, you're different. Not like any man I've ever met before. That's what I was trying to say."

"Thanks. I think." A strange grin curved one side of his mouth. "A pity your sister doesn't share those sentiments."

"What do you mean? She admires you a lot."

"Right." His sarcasm was evident.

"Truly."

"Just not enough to marry me, is all."

Certain she was dreaming, Sarah's heart skipped a beat. "Mandy told you that?" She cast a disbelieving look toward the Randolph wagon and held her breath, waiting for his reply.

"Yep. Well, no use bothering a young gal like you with my troubles, is there?" Dumping out the remains of his coffee, Jared got up and brushed off his backside, then stepped over the tongue of his wagon, exiting the circle.

Nibbling her lip, Sarah flicked a cautious glance around to make sure no one was paying them any mind. Then she gathered every ounce of gumption she possessed and rose to follow him, not even sure what she'd say. "I'm not exactly a child, you know," she blurted, flushing scarlet at being so brazen. What on earth would he think of her?

Jared, about to take a stride, stopped mid-motion and turned.

Sarah's pulse began to throb. She could barely hear over the rush in her ears. "Just because Mandy's the oldest, that doesn't mean she's the smartest. I—"

A small incredulous smile crept across the widower's mouth. He didn't move, didn't interrupt. His countenance softened considerably as he gazed down at her.

Sarah felt her insides quiver. She couldn't hold back a shuddering breath. Amanda would certainly call her to task for such boldness—but there were so few occasions to be alone with Jared Hill. And now to take a chance she never would have considered had Amanda accepted his proposal. But with her sister's rejection, he could easily turn off the trail at the next branch—and neither of them would ever see him again. Sarah pressed onward, hoping her voice and her shaking legs wouldn't fail her. "I. . .wouldn't have refused you." There. She'd said it, even if the utterance had been barely audible. Now she waited—almost prayed—for the world to open up and swallow her. She would positively die if he made light of her declaration.

He stared for a heartbeat. That merest hint of a smile reappeared as his even brows rose a notch. "Sarah. . .if you're—" He stopped, kneaded his temples, then began again. "A beautiful young girl like you—"

"Woman," she corrected bravely. *Desperately.*

"But I'm old enough—"

"To need someone who loves you," she whispered, unable to stop now without baring her soul. "And loves Bethy and Tad, too. And can't bear even the thought of having to say good-bye when we get to the end of—wherever it is we're going."

"You mean that?" he asked, appearing utterly astonished. "You'd actually settle for me? With that face of yours you could have your choice of a thousand young bucks!" He wagged his head in wonder even as undeniable hope rose in his eyes.

"My heart has already made its choice."

Jared searched her face for a moment, as if still uncertain whether to believe this was really happening. Then ever so gently, he reached toward her.

Sarah melted into his arms, barely able to hold back tears of profoundest relief as she felt his strong heart keeping pace with hers.

"I never thought for a moment I could have you," he said softly, cradling the back of her head in his palm as he rocked her in his embrace. "I figured, I mean, with you being young, you deserve somebody just starting out in life, same as you. Your sister didn't seem as taken up with fellows her age."

"Does that mean you might grow to love me, too, someday?"

His embrace tightened as he hugged her closer. "It means I won't have to go on fighting the feelings I've had for you since the first time I saw you with my young'uns. When I was sure I'd never have this chance."

Sarah turned her face up to his with a slightly teary smile. "Life's filled with chances, isn't it?"

"It is at that, Sarah Jane. It is at that." And Jared's lips at last claimed hers.

☙

Seth stared up at the midnight sky. It seemed as if every star that had ever been created was out tonight, each of them representing one of the countless ways he'd been a fool. If he lived to be a hundred he would never forget the sight of Amanda's cart turning off the trail.

Or the anguish in her eyes on that day at the river.

He turned in his bedroll, seeking comfort in the stillness while Red was on watch. What had possessed him that he'd railed at her after she'd nearly drowned? Thinking back on the event, he realized those had been the last words he'd spoken— no, bellowed—to her. After that, she'd given him a wide berth. And he sure didn't blame her.

But Amanda should have known he'd reacted out of anger. Anger at the Green for wrecking her wagon, nearly wiping out everything she owned in this world. And maybe foremost, anger at the fact widower Hill was paying her so much attention.

But there was one thing she couldn't have known. He had only now come to where he could admit it himself. He loved her.

Loved her.

He'd set ridiculous standards after Liza dumped him. They had him scrutinizing a woman against some insane checklist. Truthful? Check. Reliable? Check. Sensitive? He deflated his lungs in exasperation. What were all those traits anyway, compared to spunk, an unquenchable spirit, or a valiant heart?

Come to think of it, Seth realized, there was nothing he didn't like about Amanda Shelby. Including her faith. In its utter simplicity, it took him back to his own roots, when his deepest desire was to do justly, love mercy, and walk humbly with his God, as the Old Testament said. Since he'd turned his back on the Lord, his life had been nothing but a sham. Amanda, not Liza, was the example of true Christianity . . .and much too good for the likes of him. Maybe it was for the best that she ended up with someone else. After all, he'd practically pushed her into Jared Hill's arms himself!

Seth waited for the pain of that thought to subside.

It would take some time before the emptiness would go away, though. And inside, he knew where he had to go for the strength to live the rest of his life without her. Easing out of his blankets, he knelt beneath the stars and sought forgiveness from the God of his youth.

twenty

April 1849

"Do I look all right, Sissy? Oh, I'm still so thin."

Standing in the Randolphs' spare bedroom, which she and her sister had shared through the winter months, Amanda had to fight tears as she fluffed out Sarah's veil. Throughout the long trek over the Oregon Trail she had envisioned life with the two of them together, running a store. . .for several years, at least, if not forever. But God's plans had proven to be vastly different from hers. She would content herself with the few months that dream had been reality.

"He'll be rendered speechless," Amanda finally murmured, mustering a smile. Her fingertips lightly touched a cluster of seed pearls and alabaster sequins adorning the fitted lace bodice. "You've done a beautiful job on your gown. Maddie would be pleased to see how those years of stitching and samplers paid off."

Sarah covered Amanda's hand with hers. "I only wish I weren't moving away. Won't you please reconsider closing the shop and coming with us to Mount Shasta?" she pleaded. "Jared always said you were more than welcome. And you know how Bethy and Tad became enamored of you while they stayed here and Jared went off to find a place of our own."

With a stoic smile, Amanda met the younger girl's shimmering eyes in the oval cheval glass. "Not just yet. It's so convenient here on the farm, with Sacramento only a few miles away. You know how busy we've been, what with that tide of newcomers pouring west. Mr. Randolph doesn't seem to mind my using the wagon to drive to town and back every day—and besides, you need some time to be alone with that new little family of yours. You're a bride, remember?"

"I. . .sometimes feel a little guilty about that," Sarah confessed quietly. "After all, he did ask you first." Taking a fold of the lacy skirt in hand, she stepped away from the mirror and sat on the multihued counterpane draping the four-poster.

Amanda eased gently onto the rocker, so as not to crush the cerulean taffeta gown she wore. "Well, it's time to put those feelings to rest. You and I both know I never loved him in that way. And *I* could hardly miss seeing that *you* did."

A light pink tinted her sister's delicate cheekbones.

Increasingly conscious that soon enough the buckboard would bring Jared and his children, Amanda was determined to keep the mood light. . .the last sweet moments before Sarah's wedding ceremony would bring the younger girl's old life to an end and embark her upon the new. "It'll be ever so exciting," she gushed. "I wonder what your house looks like. I'm surprised Jared was able to finish it so quickly."

"Probably not quite as grand as this one, I'd venture. He wouldn't even give me a hint in his letters—and no doubt the little ones have been sworn to secrecy, too. I only hope the curtains I've sewn will fit the windows. It'll be nice having those braided rugs Mrs. Randolph taught me how to make, though, and the pretty needlepoint pillows you've done. But no matter what, I'm determined to like it—and to be the best wife and stepmother in the world. Perhaps one day the Lord will see fit to bless me with a child of my own."

Amanda felt tears welling deep inside. Tomorrow the shop in town would seem unbearably quiet and empty without Sarah's bubbliness. Happy as she was for her sister, it was difficult to dismiss the waves of sad reality that insisted upon washing over her.

The sound of approaching wagon wheels drifted from the lane leading into the rolling section of land.

Sarah sprang to her feet. "He's here!" she whispered breathlessly, and moved to peer out the window.

"Don't let him see you," Amanda teased. "I'll go downstairs and find out if everything's ready."

There was a soft rap on the door. Mrs. Randolph opened it and peeked around the jamb. "It'll be just a few minutes, my dears." Her glance fell upon the bride, and her eyes misted over. She stepped inside the room. "Oh, now, just look at my sweet Sarah. Almost too purty to look at, I swear. I couldn't be prouder of you if I was your own ma."

Sarah Jane flew into the older woman's arms. "Don't you dare make me cry. I'll spoil your pretty new dress."

"Pshaw!" Mrs. Randolph clucked her tongue. "Don't pay me no mind, even if some of my mountain of happiness spills out of these old eyes." She switched her attention to Amanda, slowly assessing her from head to toe. "And my other sweet gal. Never were spring flowers as purty as the two of you."

Barely containing her own emotions, Amanda joined the huge hug.

Mrs. Randolph's bosom rose and fell as she tightened the embrace, then stepped back. "I'd imagine everybody's in the right spot by now. I'll go tell Cora to start the organ. Nelson Junior never told us his wife could play."

As the first reedy notes drifted to their ears, Amanda moved to the top landing. Her eyes grew wide at the breathtaking transformation of the staircase and parlor. While she and Sarah had been fussing with curls and gowns, masses of brilliant orange poppies and blue lupine had been gathered to fill garlands, vases, and centerpieces to near overflowing. Here and there, tall tapers lent a golden aura of candlelight to the lovely scene. Taking one of the nosegays of spring beauties that Mrs. Randolph had thoughtfully left on the hall table, Amanda slowly started down, aware that all eyes in the house were upon her.

Hair slicked back and in his Sunday best, Charlie Randolph

met her at the bottom landing and offered an arm, then escorted her toward the fireplace, where Jared Hill, in a crisp new shirt and black suit, waited with the minister. Bethany and Tad, seated off to one side with Mrs. Randolph, waved and smothered giggles.

Amanda took her place, then watched Jared flick his attention toward the top of the stairs to his bride. His expression of awe almost shattered her fragile composure. It was all she could do to hold herself together as Mr. Randolph escorted Sarah Jane to the side of her husband-to-be.

Lost in remembrances of all that had transpired to bring this moment about, Amanda witnessed the simple ceremony as if it were a dream. . .a blur of loving looks, tender smiles and murmured vows, the breathless kiss. Soft laughter at the end brought her back to reality. She blinked away threatening tears and fortified herself to extend her best wishes to the newlyweds. "Much happiness," she managed to whisper as she hugged Sarah.

Returning the embrace, her sister kissed Amanda's cheek. "Oh, Mandy. . .I never knew there could be so much happiness as I feel right at this moment."

Amanda moved into Jared's open arms next. "I always wanted a brother," she told him. "I'm so glad Sarah chose you. May God bless you both."

He gave a light squeeze. "I'll take care of her for you. I promise."

"I'm sure you will. Be happy. God bless you both."

He nodded. "When you come to visit, the kids will sing you a whole raft of new songs, I'll wager. They begged me to make sure she brings her guitar home with us."

Amanda's lips parted. "You really like her music?"

"Well, sure! Can't carry a tune in a bucket, myself, but Sarah's pretty voice pleasures me."

Amanda had to laugh. After a lavish celebration of Mrs. Randolph's grandest fare, everyone went outside to see the newlyweds off.

Daylight was fading into a watercolor glory of muted rose and mauve as the setting sun gilded the edges of slender clouds low on the western horizon. A perfect end to a perfect day, Amanda decided. She bent to kiss Bethany and Tad, then their father swept them up into the wagon bed.

Sarah Jane threw her arms around Amanda once more, and they hugged hard for a long silent moment. Amanda knew instinctively that her sister was no more able to utter a word than she. Finally they eased apart with a teary smile. "Be happy," Amanda whispered again as Jared came to whisk his bride away.

Waving after them, watching until the wagon was but a speck in the distance, Amanda's heart was filled to bursting. She had never known such happiness.

Or such sadness.

❧

Amanda plucked her shawl from a hook by the door and tossed it about her shoulders, then grabbed the parcel containing the men's shirts she'd finished the night before. "Goodbye, Mrs. Randolph," she called out. "I'm going now."

"Take care on the road," came the older woman's answer from the backyard, where she was beating rugs on a clothesline.

Amanda drove the wagon at a leisurely pace toward the teeming settlement of Sacramento, whose level of noise and activity seemed to increase constantly. Every day brought more and more newcomers to replace those who had pulled up stakes and moved on to the next gold field. New businesses sprang up overnight in the very structures abandoned only days before. And an amazing number of lonesome, homesick men appeared at Amanda's shop on the pretext of needing a button sewed on or a tear mended. She never imagined she'd receive so many proposals! But after having her heart shattered two times already, marriage was the last thing on her mind.

Inhaling the heady scent of the spring flowers adorning the greening countryside, Amanda wondered if there were as many farther north, where Sarah had gone two weeks past. Perhaps one day soon, after the newlyweds had settled in, it might be fun to take the stage and visit. After all, the store was hers, and she could close it up whenever she took a fancy. Smiling at the thought, Amanda felt considerably more cheerful.

Dear Lord, her heart prayed. *Please watch after my dear Sarah Jane. I'm lost without my sister, my best friend, my confidant. I miss her so, yet I would never begrudge her this happiness. It still humbles me to think back on the indescribable journey You kept us through. Deserts, swamps, horrific storms, torturous mountains—to say nothing of how easily I might have drowned that day. . .*

As happened so often despite all her best efforts to the contrary, the memory of Seth Holloway intruded. Amanda had never so much as spoken his name aloud since the incident at the Green River. . .but a small, secret part of her couldn't help wondering what had become of the man. "Oh, what does it matter?" she hissed. The farm horse twitched an ear her way. Chagrined, Amanda returned her attention to the road.

Guiding the gelding along the bustling dirt streets of town, she took pride coming into view of the painted sign above her own enterprise. *Apparel and Alterations,* grand forest green letters proclaimed, then in much finer print, *A. J. Shelby, Proprietor.* She turned alongside and drove around to park in back of the small square building Mr. Randolph and Charlie had fitted with shelves and counters months ago.

Using the rear entrance, Amanda hung her floral-trimmed bonnet on a peg, then went through the swinging half-doors to the sales room. There she slid the shirred curtains apart on the front window and turned the Open sign out. . .duties she would perform every day, save Sundays, for the rest of her life. It was her lot, and what she had planned—or, nearly so, anyway. She would get used to the solitude. To help matters, she would look for a room to rent this afternoon as well, so it would no longer be necessary to burden the kind Randolphs or tie up their wagon. Thus decided, she began tidying the simple shop in readiness for the day's business.

After eating a bite at noon, Amanda walked several doors down the street to Mrs. Patterson's boarding house and put a deposit on a room that only that day had been vacated by a former tenant. Then, returning to her own shop, she tackled the ledgers.

The bell above the entrance interrupted the chore. Amanda set her quill aside and peered toward the dark figure silhouetted against the bright daylight. "How may I—?"

He removed his hat.

"W-why, Mr. Holloway!" Amanda gasped, rising to her feet.

Seth watched the blood drain from her face. He had been similarly shocked himself when, moments ago, he'd exited the Crown Hotel a few doors beyond the boarding house and glimpsed Amanda as she strolled to a clothing store up the street. He'd have recognized her anywhere, even with that long hair of hers tucked ever so primly into her bonnet.

He gave a perfunctory nod and settled for a simple greeting. "Good day," emerged on his second try.

"W-what are you doing here? I mean, you're the last person I ever—" Amanda's expression was one of utter confusion as she stood still, her mouth agape.

Another nod. Seth suddenly realized his hand was crushing his good hat and eased his grip. Lost in those glorious green eyes, he couldn't recall a word of the great speech he'd worked out so carefully in his head through the Oregon winter. He cleared his throat. "You're well?" *Great beginning, idiot!*

"Yes. . .fine. . .and you?"

"Not bad. Your sister, she's well?" It was all he could do not to roll his eyes at this inane conversation.

She nodded, then blinked quite suddenly and shook her

head as if to clear it. "What are you doing in Sacramento?"

No point beating around the bush, when the truth was so much easier to get out. He shored up his insides. "Looking for you, actually."

"I-I don't understand," she said, her fine eyebrows arching higher. "Why would you—?"

Seth raked his fingers through his hair. "Sorry, I never asked if you were busy, Miss Sh—I mean—are you? I won't take much of your time."

She frowned, still perplexed. "I'm not busy just now."

"Good." A tiny flicker of hope coursed through him. He breathed a quick prayer that the Lord would loosen his tongue. "I must have asked at a hundred gold camps if anyone had seen you or knew of you. I was just about to give up, when you appeared out of the blue, just down the street."

Her expression remained fixed.

"I've been wanting very much to apologize," he went on, "for the callous things I said that day at the river. They were rude and completely uncalled for."

Amanda moved nearer the swinging doors and sank slowly to one of the chairs occupying either side of them. "Really, Mr. Holloway, the incident has long since been forgotten, I assure you."

"Not by me, it hasn't." He paused. "Do you mind if I sit down?"

"Oh. Not at all." She indicated the other chair.

Noticing the absence of a wedding band during her gesture, Seth thought it odd, but figured her preferences were none of his business. Obviously Hill must be an addle brain, unconcerned about letting the world know she's taken. "As I was saying, I came to tell you how sorry I am. My partner seemed to take singular pleasure in pointing out what a cad I was— which is true. It's gnawed at me ever since."

"Well, pray, suffer no more, then. I accept your apology." A tiny smile softened her face, revealing a touch of her old feisty spirit. He didn't realize how much he'd missed it. Missed her.

"Splendid." Swallowing, Seth stood to his feet. "Then I won't keep you from your work any longer. Thank you for hearing me out. I wish you well."

"And you," she whispered.

Watching him cross to the door, Amanda rose, still in shock over his sudden appearance. "Mr. Holloway?" He paused, his hand on the latch, and turned.

"Since you've come so far, and all. . .might I offer you some tea?" At her rash invitation, Amanda felt her knees wobble as she rose. The whole thing seemed unreal, dreamlike.

"That would be. . .kind. Yes, thank you."

She waved toward the chair again. "I'll be only a moment. I had some brewing in the back room." Hastening there, she filled two cups and returned. By sheer determination she willed her hand not to tremble as she gave one of the cups to him. There was certainly no reason to be nervous.

"Thank you."

"I don't see any familiar faces in town," she said, noting the presence of circles under his dark eyes, a day or two's growth of beard. And his boots were dusty. He really must have been traveling. For some unaccountable reason, she thought that was sweet. Touching. She felt her face growing warm. He couldn't be the ogre she had painted him after all. His gaze, wandering about the premises, returned to her. "This your place?"

She nodded, gathering herself. "Didn't you see the sign?"

"I wasn't paying much attention."

"Oh. Well, it was Sarah's and mine, until she left."

"Left?" He raised the tea to his mouth.

"Moved, actually. To Mount Shasta, after she and Jared married."

He swallowed too quickly and choked, and some of the scalding brew spilled over on his hand. The cup crashed to the floor and shattered in a thousand pieces as russet spokes of tea stained the plank floor. He knelt to collect the shards. "How clumsy. Sorry."

Amanda was more concerned about him. "But you've burned yourself. Let me look at it." Before he could argue, she knelt beside him and took his work-roughened hand in hers. Gently she unraveled the clenched fingers, turning them this way and that to assess the reddened skin. "It's not—" she raised her lashes, finding his face mere inches from her own, "not too bad." The last words were barely audible.

She released her hold even as her face turned every bit as scarlet as his burn. Why had she been so impetuous? This man somehow managed to bring out the absolute worst in her—and had since the first time their paths had crossed a summer ago. She'd never been more humiliated. . .unless she counted those half dozen other times she'd been in his presence. She tried to regather her dignity while easing graciously back onto her chair seat.

He sputtered into a laugh. Then roared.

Hiking her chin, Amanda turned her back. Perhaps he wasn't the gentleman she'd thought she'd glimpsed mere moments ago. "I'll thank you not to make fun of me."

"Oh, I'd never make fun of you, Amanda," he said in all sincerity. "I promise you that."

It was the first time he had ever called her by her given name. And it sounded so—different, in that raspy voice of his. Her heart hammered erratically against her ribs as she turned and shyly met his gaze.

He wasn't laughing now. . .but a strange almost-smile caught at her, stealing her breath. "You truly came all this way just to see me?" she asked in wonder.

"Mostly. I'm trying to acquire some good horseflesh for my new venture, so I answer every advertisement I come across. But in my travels, I've been looking for you." He reached to brush a few stray hairs from her temple as his intense gaze focused on her eyes. "Everywhere."

Her mouth went dry. "That's—that's really—" Unable to think straight, she moistened her lips.

"I thought I could forget you, Amanda Shelby," he continued. "Tried my hardest to. Drove Red crazy with my mutterings. That day I saw you turn off the trail, I figured you would be marrying that widower. Even when I saw you today, I thought you'd become his wife by now." His face blanched. "Or someone else's. Are you promised to anyone?"

She shook her head, wondering where this was all leading, fearing the hope that it could go anywhere at all. And did she want it to? "Good." He appeared visibly relieved. "Then I might as well go for broke. If I were to stay on at the hotel here for a while—" He swallowed nervously. "What I mean is, would you be opposed to being courted? By me?"

Amanda felt suddenly lightheaded and took hold of a spindle of the chair to steady herself. "Aren't you forgetting the matter of my being—how did you put it—brainless and foolhardy, wasn't it?"

Seth had the grace to smile, though it was tinged with more than a little guilt. "I deserve that. I've been unbearably thoughtless to you. But I know now that I was way off course, Amanda. After you drove off the trail and out of my life, I had to face up to the way I'd mistreated you—and forsaken the Lord. I finally sought His forgiveness and then knew that to have true peace I needed to seek yours as well. I'm no longer the man you met in Independence. I've changed. Because of you. I'm asking for a chance to undo that bad impression I made on you. . .if you'll allow me to."

Looking at him, Amanda could see how vulnerable he was. There had been a considerable amount of ill feeling between them, but thinking back, she could recall sensing almost from the onset of the journey west that he was trustworthy and honest. He affected her in ways she'd never before experienced, stirred chords within her soul as no man she had ever known. And she felt profound inner peace about his offer, because for longer than she cared to admit, she had been in love with Seth Holloway.

All things considered, she had only one choice. . .to be honest in return. "I would be truly honored, Seth, to have you court me."

His vulnerability evaporated, leaving a fragile hopefulness in its place. He expelled a ragged breath and drew her close, close to the beating of his heart. "I promise you, Amanda, you will never be sorry."

Raising her lashes, Amanda tipped her head back, needing to glimpse again the intensity of the love he made no effort to disguise. Seeing it, she smiled.

Seth held her gaze for a heartbeat, then slowly lowered his head, until his lips were barely a breath from hers. Then with tenderest reverence, he kissed her.

Amanda felt her heart sing and wanted the moment to last forever. But all too soon he eased away.

"I've wanted to do that for a long time," he murmured huskily.

"And I wished for a long time that you had." The remark came in all honesty.

He wrapped his arms about her just as the bell above the door tinkled, announcing a customer.

Seth took a step back, and a comical spark of mischief glinted in his dark eyes. "Well, thank you kindly, miss," he said with a mock bow. "That's mighty friendly service, I must say. I'll be by later for that new shirt." With that, he exited, whistling.

Amanda smiled after him. *Yes, come back later, my love. I'll be here waiting.*

A Letter To Our Readers

Dear Reader:

In order that we might better contribute to your reading enjoyment, we would appreciate your taking a few minutes to respond to the following questions. When completed, please return to the following:

Rebecca Germany, Managing Editor
Heartsong Presents
P.O. Box 719
Uhrichsville, Ohio 44683

1. Did you enjoy reading *Valiant Heart?*
   ❑ Very much. I would like to see more books
      by this author!
   ❑ Moderately
      I would have enjoyed it more if _____

   _____

2. Are you a member of **Heartsong Presents**? ❑Yes ❑No
   If no, where did you purchase this book? _____

   _____

3. What influenced your decision to purchase this
   book? (Check those that apply.)

   ❑ Cover   ❑ Back cover copy

   ❑ Title   ❑ Friends

   ❑ Publicity   ❑ Other_____

4. How would you rate, on a scale from 1 (poor) to 5
   (superior), the cover design? _____

5. On a scale from 1 (poor) to 10 (superior), please rate the following elements.

    __Heroine   __Plot

    __Hero   __Inspirational theme

    __Setting   __Secondary characters

6. What settings would you like to see covered in **Heartsong Presents** books?_____

_____

_____

7. What are some inspirational themes you would like to see treated in future books?_____

_____

_____

8. Would you be interested in reading other **Heartsong Presents** titles?   ❏ Yes   ❏ No

9. Please check your age range:
   - ❏ Under 18   ❏ 18-24   ❏ 25-34
   - ❏ 35-45   ❏ 46-55   ❏ Over 55

10. How many hours per week do you read? _____

Name _____

Occupation _____

Address _____

City_____ State_____ Zip_____

LoveSong

Do you have a **Heartsong Presents** title that you can no longer find or a favorite that you would like to have in large print? Barbour Publishing announces six classic **Heartsong Presents** historical romances. . .now available in trade paper size.

____*Dakota Dawn* by Lauraine Snelling is the tale of a Norwegian immigrant and a North Dakota farmer whose ideal plans have been suddenly rearranged.

____*Eyes of the Heart* by Maryn Langer is about Prudence Beck who is alone in the logging country of Washington Territory and longs to make a life for her unborn child.

____*Heartbreak Trail* by VeraLee Wiggins follows Rachel's adventurous trip along the Oregon Trail, one that soon turns to sorrow.

____*A Light in the Window* by Janelle Jamison is the story of a nurse in the Alaskan wilderness whose career is threatened by a determined suitor and an outbreak of diphtheria.

____*Proper Intentions* by Dianne L. Christner is set in Ohio as the nineteenth century approaches and orphaned Kate longs for a husband and family of her own.

____*The Unfolding Heart* by JoAnn A. Grote shows what happens when a creature of comfort faces the crude and dangerous Minnesota frontier and discovers a strong love for a down-to-earth minister.

·········· Presents ··········

Great Inspirational Romance at a Great Price!

Heartsong Presents books are inspirational romances in contemporary and historical settings, designed to give you an enjoyable, spirit-lifting reading experience. You can choose wonderfully written titles from some of today's best authors like Peggy Darty, Sally Laity, Tracie J. Peterson, Colleen L. Reece, Lauraine Snelling, and many others.

When ordering quantities less than twelve, above titles are $2.95 each.
Not all titles may be available at time of order.

Heart♥ng Presents
Love Stories Are Rated G!

That's for godly, gratifying, and of course, great! If you love a thrilling love story, but don't appreciate the sordidness of some popular paperback romances, **Heartsong Presents** is for you. In fact, **Heartsong Presents** is the *only inspirational romance book club*, the only one featuring love stories where Christian faith is the primary ingredient in a marriage relationship.

Sign up today to receive your first set of four, never before published Christian romances. Send no money now; you will receive a bill with the first shipment. You may cancel at any time without obligation, and if you aren't completely satisfied with any selection, you may return the books for an immediate refund!

Imagine. . .four new romances every four weeks—two historical, two contemporary—with men and women like you who long to meet the one God has chosen as the love of their lives. . .all for the low price of $9.97 postpaid.

To join, simply complete the coupon below and mail to the address provided. **Heartsong Presents** romances are rated G for another reason: They'll arrive *Godspeed!*